# The Freak in Me

Interior Design by Saige the Gemini

For more information, or to contact authors, send correspondence to:

Rose-Antrum Empire
sthegemini69@gmail.com

Saige the Gemini

# The Freak in Me

"Eat that pussy just like that baby! Ahhhhh, I'm about to cum all over your face and in your mouth X! Keep your tongue right there, I'm about to cummmmm!!!!"

"Damn Trice, you came all over my face and everything ma," Xavier told me while reaching for a towel to wipe his face.

"Aht aht, don't blame that on me, you wouldn't let up so what was I supposed to do?"

"Yea, whatever," he said to me while stroking his dick.

"Come here and let me repay you." Xavier laid on his bed next to me; I got on my knees, placed one of his legs in between mine and went to town on his dick. Now if you know me, you know my head game is top tier.

"Trice, slow down baby, you're about to make me bust."

# The Freak in Me

"That's the point of sucking your dick, isn't it? What good is head if you don't cum from it? I asked him before getting back on his dick to finish him off.

"Trice, let me up baby, I'm bout to bust!" He said while tapping my shoulder and trying his hardest to get my lips from around his dick.

I ignored him and kept sucking, making his dick wetter, and massaging his balls while my tongue and mouth made magic.

"Fuckkk, Trice!!!" He yelled as he came all in my mouth and face. "Yo, you don't play fair at all, you get a kick outta this shit, don't you?"

In between me laughing I replied, "You know I do; we go through this every time I top you off, what makes you think this time was going to be any different?"

"Yo, something is really wrong with you," he said then began laughing.

As I was getting dressed, I asked, "What time is it?"

# Saige the Gemini

"It's quarter till five, you got somewhere to be?"

"Yea, I gotta meet the girls at five, I should be able to make it back to my dorm, shower really quick, get dressed and meet them."

"Where y'all going tonight?"
"Nowhere, we just gotta meet to discuss some stuff."

"Yea, aight," he replied with an attitude. "I'll text you when I'm done, okay?"

"Don't bother," he replied holding his dorm room door open for me?"

"Yo, whatever," I said while walking out. One thing I didn't have time for was his bullshit ass attitude, I wasn't about to let him fuck up my night when I knew it was about to get a lot more interesting as the night progressed. His bullshit ass attitude was one reason he hadn't yet met my girls and if there was a chance he was going to stick around, I'm not sure I wanted him to meet them, but only time will tell.

# The Freak in Me

My girls and I have an informational to go to so we could see if pledging Delta Pi Psi was the sorority for us. I showered, got dressed and we made it to the informational with three minutes to spare.

When we got there, it was amazing, all of the information they presented us with was perfect for me, and if I may, I'd say it was perfect for my girls as well. We were in for the time of our lives going through this pledge process for Delta Pi Psi, it was about to be a freaky, kinky good time and I was ready for all of it!

"Ladies, I thank you for taking the time out of your busy schedules to come to this informational. We are going to keep this nice, sweet, and quick as I have a dick appointment in about twenty minutes. My name is Soror Ass to Mouth or ATM for short. Soror Squirt In Ya Face already gave you the basics, if you feel as if DPP is right for you, feel free to stay, if not, you can leave now."

# Saige the Gemini

Most of the women in attendance got up and left, one of them stayed in the same dorm as I did, she looked at me with a look of disgust when she saw I wasn't leaving.

"Scared bitch," was the only thing I said to her before she left the building. She was one of those prissy bitches, she was probably still a virgin and the sight of her irked my soul, it was a good thing she decided to leave, not too sure how it would've worked out being on-line with her and having to deal with her every day.

Anyway, Soror ATM proceeded, "We will collect your information one by one then you'll be dismissed, since there are only six of you, we should be done in about five minutes or so."

Once my girls and I gave Soror ATM our information, we left and headed back to our dorm. When I got off the elevator, Xavier was sitting in the windowsill.

"I don't have the energy to argue with you Xavier."

# The Freak in Me

"I didn't come here to argue with you Trice, I missed you and wanted to spend some time with you."

Just as I was about to respond, this chick, Donise, the dorm slut came up to Xavier and said, "Damn X, you still here? You coming back for seconds?"

I laughed, and told the both of them, "Enjoy yourselves."

"X grabbed me by my arm and said, "Donise, chill the fuck out, you on the bullshit tonight, for real." The he said to me, "Trice, it's not what you think, I promise you it's not."

"Xavier, you, and I both know my mouth and pussy just gave your dick the best workout it's ever had, so stop acting like I'm lying," Donise told him.

I gently took his hand off of my arm, told them to have an amazing night and walked to my room. I sent a text to the girls, I needed a girl's night out, I changed my clothes, did my hair, and

# Saige the Gemini

met up with them so we could drive to Central since they were having a party tonight.

We all got into Kiera's truck and made our way to New Britain to party with the students at Central. We partied hard, all of the fraternities and sororities were out, but one specific fraternity stood out to my girls and I, they were wearing black and red, some of them had gold too, and their letters were BDM. I took my phone out and tried to google them, but nothing came up, I made a mental note to do more research on them.

By time we left Central and got back to our campus, it was about two in the morning, so I went straight to my room, grabbed my towel, shower shoes and toiletries, and made my way to the showers. Once I got out of the shower my phone was alerting me that I had a missed message. When I got back to my room I read the message, it said, *"Hello ladies, pledge time has started so I need you to be at the address of the informational by three-thirty am, no excuses. See you ladies in a few!"*

I called Kiera who called the other ladies, "Hey, did y'all get the message from Soror Squirt in Ya Face?" I asked them.

"Yup, we're throwing our clothes on now, if we're riding together, y'all got ten minutes to meet me at the car." Kiera said.

I had about ten minutes to get myself together and meet the girls at Kiera's truck; I wasn't trying to get left. When we all got into Kiera's car, Akira asked, "So, what do y'all think tonight is going to be like?"

"Shit if I know, did they ever tell us what the meaning behind Delta Pi Psi was?"

"Nope," Akira responded.
"Akira, I'm surprised you're pledging seeing as though your father is super against Greek life," I said to her.

"What he doesn't know won't hurt him. It was a struggle to get him to let me move on campus, my mother and I had to damn near move mountains to make that happen so as long as I can stay under the radar with this pledging thing, I'll be good until after we cross, then I'll tell him."

"It has to suck having a strict ass father, I'm glad I don't know who my father is cause he'd probably be the same way," Kiera joked.

"Yo, something is really wrong with you," I said to Kiera laughing.

When we pulled up to the location, Soror ATM was standing outside; we were early so that was a good thing.

"Ladies are you ready for your first night of your initiation into Delta Pi Psi?" she asked us.

We all responded simultaneously, "hell yea!"

"Alright ladies, tonight, we're going to get kinky, a little freaky and downright nasty. Tonight you will see why we are the number one erotic sorority around. If you are in a relationship, we think it's best for you to keep your involvement with Delta Pi Psi under wraps until the initiation process is over with as you will be engaging in activities that will undoubtedly put your relationship at risk."

As soon as Ass To Mouth said that my girls and I all looked at Akira, she was the only one of us who was in a committed relationship with the love of her life, Justice.

Soror ATM continued, "ladies, tonight, we are going to be uninhibited, free sexual beings, and we are going to do it with the help of some of the sexiest men from the number one erotic fraternity around, Beta Delta Mu. Ladies get ready to suck some dicks, eat some pussy, bust that pussy and ass open for these men, are y'all ready?"

We looked at one another in pure shock, our jaws dropped, and eyes were wide open.

Soror ATM repeated, "I said are you ladies ready for tonight? If you're having second thoughts and don't think DPP is right for you, you can leave now."

We looked at one another again and responded together, "Yes we're ready!"

"Great, now let the fun begin! Each guy has been assigned to two of you, and there are rooms in the back, each room has your name on it, so find your room and let's get down and dirty tonight!"

I walked down the hall to the back of the building, found my room, my name was up there with Kiera's and when we opened the door, there was this dark skinned, tall, beautiful man.

"Hello beautiful ladies, my name is Antoine, are y'all ready for an amazing night?"

My eyes were fixated on his third leg, I never ran from a dick before but tonight may be the night it happens, just the sight of it had me second-guessing this initiation.

"Hello Antoine, my name is Kiera, and this is my friend Trice."

# The Freak in Me

"Well ladies, let's start having some fun."

Antoine started kissing on my thighs, Kiera started licking his dick, and when he got fully erect, oh my black Jesus, his dick was huge. I laid on the bed, Kiera laid on top of me and began kissing me, and then, Antoine slowly entered into me.

"Fuck," was all I could say at first, his dick was stretching me out something serious.

"Do you need me to stop?" he asked me.

"No, please don't, I can take it."

After a few strokes, I was able to get adjusted to Antoine's dick. After a good half-hour nonstop, Antoine had worn my pussy out, and now it was Kiera's turn. Her face told it all, she was taken aback by Antoine's width and length just as I was. While Kiera was getting her pussy worked out by Antoine, I was getting my pussy licked by her, which I desperately needed because he had put a hurting on my lady parts.

## Saige the Gemini

I think I was Kiera's first girl experience, but she definitely wasn't mine, and to be her first, she knew what she was doing, and she did it very well. After an hour and a half of pure nastiness, dick sucking, pussy eating, ass fucking, sadly, our night with Antoine was ending. Kiera and I got ourselves together, I slid Antoine my number just in case he wanted seconds with me, and we left; all of the other ladies were already at Kiera's truck waiting for us.

"Damn, y'all look like you had the time of your lives!" Akira said laughing.

"Oh we did, we absolutely did," I told them laughing.

"Well listen, y'all come through to my room whenever y'all get up and get yourselves together so we can talk about our first night of initiation."

# The Freak in Me

"Is eleven good for every one? We can order brunch and catch up on the events of tonight."

"Eleven sounds good, now let's go so we can shower and get some sleep!"

We finally got back to our dorms around quarter after four and as soon as I got to my room, I grabbed my shower necessities and made my way to the shower.

## The next morning

I woke up around quarter after ten which gave me enough time to shower, get dressed and make it over to Akira's room to have brunch and talk about the amazing first night of our initiation.

We ordered brunch from Bella's, poured us some mimosas, and got to dish about how our night went.

# Saige the Gemini

"Yooooo, last night was crazy!! Like where the hell did they find these men with these third legs, hurricane tongues, and crazy ass stamina?" Akira asked.

"Your guy had a third leg too? Ours had me stuck, like mouth wide open. I ain't never been scared of a dick but shit, last night, he had me shook!" I told them.

Jade responded, "Ours had a third leg, hurricane tongue and the body of a god."

"What's up with these guys from Beta Delta Mu? Was anyone able to get the scoop on them? I keep seeing guys around campus with the letters, but I don't want to go up to any of them and ask them what's really good with their fraternity," Akira asked.

"Nah, but I heard there are chapters all over, and I heard they are big time in the south, like bigger than some of the other fraternities," I responded.

# The Freak in Me

As soon as I said that Akira's eyes got big, I feel like she might've been thinking about Justice being in school in Georgia, so I had to ease her mind just a little.

"Akira, I'm sure you have nothing to worry about, you know how Justice feels about you, y'all are relationship goals for me, and all of us here knows that Justice would never do anything to jeopardize your relationship."

"Do y'all think he would step out on me like these guys last night if he ever did decide to pledge Beta Delta Mu?"

Kiera responded, "Akira, did you really just ask us this? After everything you were just doing in that room last night with the guy with the third leg and hurricane tongue?"

"Kiera, really?! This is not the time for this!!" I told her slapping her arm gently.

"I hate to be the devil's advocate here, but I have to agree with Kiera, I mean shit, if Justice were to pledge BDM and if it were anything like we were doing last night, would you not want him to join the fraternity? You do realize the benefits of joining a fraternity and sorority, right? Lifelong connections, better job and business opportunities, and the list goes on," Jade said.

"You know what, y'all can get the fuck up outta my room!" Akira yelled at us.

"Yo, really? Are you really kicking us outta your room?" I asked stunned as hell.

"Yup, all of you can get the fuck outta my room, please and thank you!"

We all grabbed our things, food for the walk back to our respective dorms as well as mimosas and got up outta her room.

Kiera said to us as we were walking to our rooms, "be serious with me y'all, did I say something that wasn't legitimate?"

"I responded, not at all, but you know how sentimental she is about Justice and the mere thought of him being inside of another female, shit, she doesn't even like other women looking at him, so you know she'd be sick of the thought of him fuckin' other chicks just to get initiated into a fraternity."

"As long as I didn't say anything other than the truth, I can handle her attitude, but she can't be going on and on about a dude with a third leg and hurricane tongue but be mad at the possibility of Justice doing the same thing while pledging a fraternity."

"Trust me Kiera, I get it and I understand it. I'm going to see y'all later, I'm about to go to the room, eat, enjoy the last of these mimosas and get to working on my English paper."

"Alright boo, we will see you later!" Jade said before hugging me and making her way to her dorm.

When I got to my room, the last person I wanted to see was standing at my door waiting for me, Xavier.

"What the hell are you doing here X?"

"Can we go in your room and talk? We didn't leave things on a good note yesterday."

"Make it quick, I have things to do today."

We walked into my room, I sat on my bed and Xavier sat at my desk.

"Trice, you know I love you, right?"

"I know what you say but your words and actions don't mix, what the fuck was that shit yesterday with that hoe Donise?"

"It was nothing Trice, I told you that shit yesterday right in front of her."

"And I call bullshit, you don't even realize that you tensed up when you saw her coming and your palms were sweaty when she mentioned you coming back for seconds."

He exhaled deeply then said, "listen Trice, it was an accident, it wasn't supposed to go down the way it did, it was just supposed to be her and I studying since we're in the same tech class."

# The Freak in Me

"And let me guess, you just happened to slip into her pussy and couldn't find your way out?"

"Nah, not even, we were studying, and drinking, she had music playing and the next thing I know she was topping me off and before I knew it, we were fucking. I promise you baby, I never intended on it happening."

"I hope y'all make each other happy X, I truly do, now I'm going to have to ask you to leave my room and my life for good, I refuse to allow you to humiliate me more than you have already."

"Trice, can we have an adult conversation about this please?"

"Nah, you good, I need you to leave, I have a paper to write," I told him while escorting him out of my room.

He left, and as I closed my door, I heard Donise saying something to him and he

# Saige the Gemini

responding, I laughed and went on and started on my paper that was due at midnight.

# Later that night...

I finished my paper at ten thirty and it seemed like as soon as I hit send to email it to my professor, I got a message from Soror SIYF, and it read, *"Good evening ladies, it's time for your second night of initiation, but tonight, it's the ladies for the ladies. Tonight, we won't have any extra people for the fun tonight, there are six of you, so therefore, it's every woman for us all, how nasty can y'all really get with one another. The address for tonight's fuckstevities is 3006 Dixwell Ave, Hamden, see you beauties at 12:30am."*

"Oh this should be fun, fun, fun," I said aloud.

Kiera called me as soon as she got the text, "Yo bitch, I'm on the other side of town and won't make it back to campus to pick y'all up for this initiation thing tonight."

"That's cool hoe, Jade and I will most likely ride together."

"What about Akira and the others?"
"Have you spoken to Akira since that shit earlier? I'm respectfully giving her the space she wanted after she kicked us outta her room."

"Nah, I haven't heard from her, maybe Kyra will let the others ride with her, either way, I'm going to shower really quick, get dressed and be out."

"Aight sis, I'll see y'all when we get there," she said to me before hanging up.

Before I went to take my shower, I sent Jade a quick message asking if she wanted to ride with me to the fuckstevities, she responded right back that she was down and she'd be at my room within the next fifteen minutes, which gave me enough time to shower, and start getting ready.

"Ladies, first off let me say thank you for being prompt, one thing I can't stand is when people are late. As you've read in the text that was sent to you there will be no others in attendance tonight, just the six of you. We want to see how nasty, freaky, and uninhibited you ladies can get with one another. If you haven't been with women before, I'm happy you're going to pop your cherry with one of your future line sisters."

"We will not break into different rooms as we want you to feel free to move from partner to partner if you'd like. The other rooms are open just in case you feel more comfortable being in a secluded area; we want you to feel comfortable while getting your freak on. Any questions?" Soror ATM added.

No one said anything but I could tell that some of the other ladies were a little nervous about tonight's fuckstevities than I was; it was all over their faces. Akira made eye contact with me, I guess it was her way of saying that he wanted to be paired up with me, and I think both Sorors ATM & SIYF noticed it too.

"Okay ladies, you will be paired up as follows, Jade and Marie, Kiera and Trice, Akira & Kyra; and remember, you're not obligated to stay with the person you're partnered with, so ladies, it's time to get sexy and kinky with one another!"

We all mutually decided to play together, Kiera came over and attempted to kiss me, but she was a little hesitant, so I helped her out. I pushed her hair behind her ear, and then I kissed her softly, one hand on her face and one hand on unbuttoning her blouse. I took her blouse off, unbuttoned her bra, her titties looked so good.

I put one hand on her neck and put my head in between her legs, I kissed her on the inside of both of her thighs and proceeded to tongue kiss her clit.

# Saige the Gemini

"Fuck Trice!"

"You like what I'm doing to you?"

"Hell yea! You eating the fuck outta that pussy, oh my gawd!"

"Tell me how much you love my mouth on your pussy sis."

"I love it, you are the best pussy eater ever Trice."

"That's what I like to hear."

As I was eating Kiera out, Marie and Akira came behind me, pulled my leggings down and Marie began fingering my already wet pussy. My eyes began to roll into the back of my head; she was a pro at this shit. Jade got naked and sat on top of Kiera's face and Kyra positioned herself so Jade could eat her out when she was being eaten.

Off to the side, Akira had gone solo and was fingering herself as she watched the rest of us doing our thing, and before I knew it Sorors Ass to Mouth and Squirt in Ya Face had joined the party and were doing their own thing as well.

# The Freak in Me

The room was full of sex, and I wasn't at all mad about it, all of this was almost making me miss Xavier, almost. Three hours later, we were all spent and orgasmed out, we got ourselves dressed and made our way back to our dorms.

Once I got to my dorm I showered and went straight to bed, a bitch was tired as fuck.

Ten in the morning my alarm went off, I almost forgot I had a noon class. I got myself together and made it to class. As I'm sitting in my communications class my phone began buzzing like crazy. The messages were from Soror ATM, she was praising us for the night before, she was telling us how she was inspired by us. She then sent me a private text message asking if we could maybe link up on the side one evening. I left her message on read, I had to think about it because Soror ATM was one fine bitch, and if I liked pussy as much as I loved dick, she'd be my bitch.

Once I left my communication's class, I stopped by the café to grab something to eat, I tried to stay away from the school's café, but I hadn't yet gone grocery shopping, so I had no choice but to grab something really quick.

# The Freak in Me

As I was leaving, I ran into Xavier and Donise.

"Damn," I heard Xavier say when he saw me.

"Don't y'all look cute together," I said to the both of them.

"Trice, it's not what it looks like, I promise you it's not."

"Xavier, I'm not trippin', I'm really not, I hope y'all enjoy the rest of your day, I gotta go."

Seeing Xavier and Donise together didn't faze me, I think I was beginning to be over him for good. When I got to my room I ate, put some music on and started my homework. Just as I was about to submit my homework for my communications class, there was a knock at my door.

"It's open!" I yelled out to the person on the other side of my door.

"Hey beautiful," Xavier said.

# Saige the Gemini

I immediately regretted the fact that I didn't get up and see who was on the other side of the door.

"How can I help you?"

"You don't sound like you're happy to see me."

"It's because I'm not happy, what do you want X?"

"I want us to talk, I want us to get to a better place with one another, I miss us, and I want us to work."

I hit submit for my homework, turned to look at Xavier and gave him my undivided attention.

"Go ahead and talk X, you have my full undivided attention."

"Listen Trice, I love you and I want us to make this relationship work, I know I've fucked up too many times to count, with Donise being my latest fuck up, we only fucked once and that was because you and I had an argument. She's hell bent on making you jealous and making you believe that there is more going on between the both of us than there is. I have plans on marrying you one day, I don't want to lose you Trice, I love you more than life."

"Xavier, I love you too but how much shit am I supposed to take from you and how many times am I supposed to be humiliated by you? Is humiliation and disrespect apart of being in a relationship with you? Do you know how many times I've been walking around campus having to hear all the rumors about the two of you? Do you realize how embarrassing that shit is? Like when is enough really enough?"

"I understand that Trice, I really do, and I will do anything and everything to make it up to you and to get us back on track. What can I do to get back on track with you and make this work for the both of us?"

"I think we need to take a break for a while, I need to focus on school right now and some other things I have going on in my life. Hopefully we can reconnect and rekindle our relationship once you get your cheating ways out of your system."

"Trice, are you sure you want to take a break from our relationship?"

"Yes, I'm sure. Every time I've seen you around campus, it's been you and Donise together, got people looking at me like I'm crazy because they know you're supposed to be in a relationship with me. It's blatant disrespect, and I'm too good of a woman to be played with and have my feelings not taken into consideration, you have a lot of growing up to do and you seem to still want to have your cake and eat it too, so until you know how to be monogamous, you can do you and I'm going to do me."

He looked so defeated, but I needed my peace and seeing him and that bitch Donise parading around campus like they were a couple, it was stressing me out, it was embarrassing, and it was time for me to find my happy.

"I understand, I'm sorry to keep hurting you and I really hope that one day we can get back together and live our lives together and happy."

We hugged; he kissed me on my cheek, and walked out of my room.

I sent a group text to the ladies and told them I needed a girl's night in, getting rid of Xavier was a breath of fresh air but I needed my girls just in case I had a minor meltdown.

We all met up at Jade's room, my girls cooked for us, we had drinks food, and games, it was just what I needed to get over Xavier.

"So Trice, are you and X really a done deal?" Kyra asked me.

"Yea, I'm good on him. He and Donise keep parading around campus like they're a couple and making me look crazy, so therefore, I'm good on him, he can fuck whomever he wants to and not have to feel guilty about doing it."

"I think you should meet Justice's brother, JayVon, I think he's more your speed," Kiera said.

"Nah, I'm good on relationships for a while, I'm focusing on school and making sure I get into Delta Pi Psi, anything else will be a distraction that I don't need right now."

"I think if you meet him and really get to know him, you'll change your mind." "Maybe, but right now my focus is DPP, speaking of, have y'all heard anything else from any of the big sisters? I'm ready for our next task."

"I bet you are hoe."
"Listen sistas, I'd love to stay here with y'all but a bitch got a date tonight," Kyra said to us.

"It's all good sis, go do you and be safe, hit us in the group chat when you've made it back safely," I told her hugging her.

Jade turned some 90s music on and we

# The Freak in Me

danced and drank the rest of the night away; this was just what the doctor ordered.

## Later that night...

Around one in the morning I got a text message from Kyra saying she needed to talk to me, I told her to come down to my room, I left the door unlocked for her.

"You good boo?"

"Hell no I ain't good! That mothafucka Jarrod tried to fuckin rape me tonight!"

"Wait, what? Did you call the police or report him?"

"No, I tried to gut him like a fish, didn't want to cops to see what I tried to do to him, had to change my clothes and everything in my car cause they were covered in blood. He's currently at the hospital trying to get stitched up and save whatever is left of his dick, fuckin' bastard."

"Listen, if you need to stay here for a few

nights, you're more than welcomed to."

"I appreciate you Trice, more than you know."

I gave her a brand new pair of pajama shorts and top that I just bought a few days ago; the extra bed in my room had freshly washed linen on them. Kyra undressed and the sight of her perfectly round ass, and the way her breasts were perfect, it had me wondering how she tasted.

"Trice, Kiera told me how you rocked her body right the other night," she told me sitting on the bed across from me naked.

"Oh is that right? What else did she tell you?" I asked moving closer to her.

"You really have a way with using your mouth, the way you made her feel, she said she's starting to second guess if she's really into men or not."

"So, is that your way of telling me you want to see if I can rock your pussy like I did hers?"

# The Freak in Me

"It is, and this can be our little secret, the rest of the girls don't need to know anything about this."

"Our secret is safe with me," I told her as I undressed, and gently parted her thighs.

We kissed passionately, her hand gripping my ass, my hands gripping her breast.

As each second passed by we got wetter and wetter, we were going to have fun tonight.

"Trice, you got me so wet right now, fuck!" "You ain't seen nothing yet baby girl," I told her while fingering her pussy.

I planted small kisses on her neck, then moved down to her breasts, kissing and sucking on each one of her nipples, from her breasts, I moved further south, until I got to her sweet spot. I started out licking her pussy, then sucked on her clit gently, the moans she was making let me know she was thoroughly enjoying my mouth on her. My hands cupped both of her breasts, and she arched her back up, she began grinding her hips while I was eating her out, she tapped me on my shoulder, then said, "let me taste you now."

We switched positions, and she went straight for the kill; I was already wet but she brought the tsunami out of me, I don't know what type of magical shit she was doing to my pussy, but Kyra had me squirting, squirming and tapping out.

After Kyra damn near drowned herself in my wetness, she positioned herself on top of me, her pussy rubbing against mine she had me going crazy. Just as we were about to climax together, she kissed me deeply, which made the climax even stronger, we both screamed out in ecstasy.

"Kyra, you don't play fair, you must do this on the regular," I told her while grabbing my robe and shower caddy.

"Honestly, you're the first female I've really been with except for our first initiation task."

# The Freak in Me

"Ain't no fucking way I'm the first you've been with!"

"I'm serious Trice, I watch a lot of pornos, so that's where I kinda learned how to do what I do. Did you enjoy yourself?"

I looked at her like she was delirious then pointed to the large wet spot on the bed then said; "I almost drowned you in my wetness, that wet bed says I enjoyed myself more than ever."

"Good, I'm glad you enjoyed yourself, I enjoyed you as well," she responded while grabbing her toiletries and a towel.

We headed to the shower and we started round two, we got into the same shower stall, I dropped down into a squatting position and began eating her out, she had one hand on the wall and the other holding up both of her breasts so she could lick and suck on them as I was making mouth love to her pussy. The moans from the both of us echoed in the bathroom, and when we climaxed together, I was certain we

## Saige the Gemini

would break the glass. We showered, went back to my room and called it a late morning.

## Two days later...

It was five in the morning and I got a text message saying that I needed to be at the warehouse within the next twenty minutes, I got up, showered quickly, got in my car and made my way to the warehouse. I didn't have time to see who was riding with who so I hoped and prayed the ladies got the message and was on their way.

When I pulled up to the warehouse I noticed there was only one other car there and it didn't belong to any of my girls, so I wondered what was going on. I walked into the warehouse and there was Soror ATM, dressed in only a bra and a thong.

"Welcome Trice, I'm glad you were able to make it."

"Thank you big sis ATM, am I early?"

# The Freak in Me

"No, you're right on time; you were the only one to get the message to be here this morning. I've had my eyes on you since the beginning of your initiation process and you are the perfect fit for Delta Pi Psi, you are everything we embody and then some."

"Wow, thank you for such a compliment, but I'm still a little confused as to why it's only the two of us here."

"Well, myself and Soror SIYF have talked about you and the other ladies and we've come to the mutual decision that we'd like to unofficially welcome you to Delta Pi Psi Sorority, Incorporated."

"Wait, is this a joke?" I asked her looking around the warehouse for all of the other big sisters to pop out and yell, "Gotcha!"

"Yes Trice, or should I address you by your line name, Soror Porn Star," she told me smiling.

I took a seat, I had to process this, and then I looked up to her and said, "what about the other ladies? Are they in as well? We're in this together and I don't want to make them feel any type of way."

"They will be just fine, you just worry about yourself," she told me while walking slowly towards me, then stopping right in front of me.

I wanted to take her right then and there but I didn't want to overstep my bounds.

Soror ATM bent over and kissed me, she tasted like fresh mint, she took me by my hand, stood me up and then said, "You can be done with your initiation process with one last task, are you up for the challenge?"

Without hesitation, I responded, "Absolutely."

"Follow me," she said.

We walked to the other side of the warehouse; there were two guys in the room, they had masks on, I had no clue as to who they were or what they looked like.

# The Freak in Me

"Trice, these two men are apart of your last initiation task, you will have fifteen minutes to make both of them cum, and from what they've told me, they don't cum easily."

"One things for sure and two for certain, I don't back down from a challenge. Are you gentlemen ready?"

They nodded their heads in the affirmative and quickly dropped their pants. One of the guys was hung, he had the biggest dick I've yet to see. I decided I'd save him for last, the other guy was average, and I felt in my heart that getting him to cum would be an easy task.

I stood up, took all my clothes off, started playing with my pussy, she was wet, dripping wet; I slipped a condom on to the first guys dick and within the first two minutes, he was cumming all in the condom, I could tell that when he fucked, if he even fucked, he was a quick pumper.

# Saige the Gemini

He stood up, grabbed his clothes and mumbled the word 'bitch' as he was leaving, I laughed, it wasn't my fault he couldn't control his dick.

This next guy, he was rock hard already, so I slipped a condom onto him, and as much as I don't want to admit this to y'all, but at first, I couldn't fit his whole dick into my mouth, this was a first for me. His dick was like two and half of Xavier's put together, and the width, fuckin' bananas.

I started off slow, relaxing, and making sure I was breathing through my nose. Once I finally got relaxed and got into a groove, homeboy started to get a little antsy, it was at that moment I knew I had him right where I needed him. My mouth and tongue making love to his dick and my hands massaging his balls, making sure to get them as wet as possible, one thing I knew about myself was that my head skills were top tier.

# The Freak in Me

I'm not sure how long I was making mouth love to his dick, but I know just as he was about to bust, he took the condom off and came all over my breasts.

The mystery man took his mask off and I'll be damned if he didn't look exactly like Justice, Akira's man.

"Damn ma, I've had a lot of women bless my dick, but none quite compare to you. Did Soror ATM say your name was Trice?"

"Yea, or you can call me Soror Porn Star, and your name is?" I asked him while cleaning myself up and getting dressed.

"I'll be whomever you want me to be, but my name is JayVon, or you can call me Pussy Monster."

"Hmm, JayVon, you have a rep here at ECU, I've heard about you."

"Huh, is that right? You have me curious as to what you've heard about me."

# Saige the Gemini

"Surprisingly, nothing bad, some of my girls feel as if we'd make a cute couple for some reason."

"What girls of yours think we should be together?"

"Which ones don't matter, I'm just shocked to see you over in these parts, don't you go to school in Georgia?"

"Yea, but my brother and one of our cousins is here for the weekend to handle some business, we fly back out tomorrow morning."

"That's what's up, well, have a safe flight back home Jay," I told him while making my way to the parking lot.

He quickly grabbed his belongings, and walked me to my car. Just as he was about to ask me something, Soror ATM got out of her car and walked over to us.

"Soror Porn Star, it is with great honor I welcome you to Delta Pi Psi Sorority", she told me while handing me my line jacket, paddle, two shirts and lapel pin.

I stood there in disbelief and started crying a little, and then I asked, "what about the others? Are they in as well? I don't want any bad blood between us and I can't stomach being in the sorority without my girls, it's either all of us or none of us."

"As I told you earlier, they're good, just make sure you keep todays fuckstivities on the low, and don't let them see your paraphernalia; and lastly, you're officially done with your initiation process but you're more than welcomed to attend the last couple of sessions and you will have to be in attendance to the probate when we announce the newest members of the sorority."

"Totally understandable, and thank you again Soror ATM and please send my gratitude to Soror SIYF for me."

"Will do", she responded, then she turned to JayVon and said, "Pussy Monster, I thank you for taking time out of your busy schedule and helping with this initiation process, you are appreciated," she told him then planted a kiss on his cheek.

"The pleasure was all mine," Jay told her while winking at me.

"Well, I have things to do, the two of you be safe and get to your destinations safe, and Trice, you'll be hearing from us soon."

Soror ATM left, and Jay looked at me and said, "What are your plans for the rest of the evening?"

"I'm not sure yet, I don't have any classes, I might just catch up on some sleep and do some research on this business idea I've been sitting on for a few months."

"Word? Where's your phone?"

I handed him my phone, he called his phone from mine and saved my number as I saved his. He then said, "if you need an ear for your business idea, give me a call or we can video chat, I'm a business major so I can probably be an asset to you."

"Oh, is that right? Quiet as it's kept, I'm a business major as well, but I still might take you up on your offer to bounce off some ideas to you."

"I'll be waiting to hear from you beautiful," he told me while opening my car door for me.

"So, Trice, it's been two weeks since we've met and I've told you all about my life, family and you have yet to divulge any information about your family."

"Aren't we nosy?"

"Nah, more like interested in getting to know you on a deeper level."

"Well, where should I start? My aunt and uncle raised me since I was like two weeks old, my parents were young, irresponsible, and weren't at all ready to be parents, so my moms older sister, who was already married, and trying to conceive, took me and raised me as her own, and I attribute everything to her because only Black Jesus knows how I would've turned out. Oh! Before I forget to tell you, I'll be in Georgia in a few days, my aunt lives down there and her birthday is the end of the week and I never miss an opportunity to spend her birthday with her."

# The Freak in Me

"Well you know if you're coming to my state we're going to have to hang out at least one day, if you're available."

"Why did you think I told you I was coming to town? I wouldn't dare come to Georgia and not link up with you."

"I'm excited now cause quiet as it's kept, I've been missing you."

"How and we just met like two and a half weeks ago?"

"I know but there's something about you that has me intrigued. Yo, are you the first in your family to be in a sorority?"

"Confession, I kinda been missing you too, and to answer your question, I think I'm the first in my family to be in a sorority, but I'm not one hundred percent sure, that's one of the things I want to talk to my aunt about when I get there, she has a ton of pictures and old ass VHS tapes from back in the day so while I'm there I'm going to go through her pictures and hopefully find a VCR and find out more about my birth parents."

"Well listen, if you want some company while going through all of the pictures and tapes, I'll be a phone call or text away."

"I appreciate you Jay, I really do, and you know I'm going to take you up on your offer."

"You better and I appreciate you too. Listen shorty, I'm bout to go out with my brother and some of our guys, if you need me, just text me."

"You go ahead and have fun with your people, I'll hit you up when I get to Georgia in a few days."

"Alright love, I'll see you when you get here, be safe and hit me as soon as you land."

"Okay love, I'll talk to you soon."

# The Freak in Me

## Three Days Later...

*"Hey love, I just touched down in Atlanta, I'm picking my rental up and I'll be at my aunt's house, her address is 3191 Hogan St, Atlanta. Hope to hear from you soon."*

As soon as I got to my aunt's house, Jay called me.

"What's up luv?"

"Nothing much, just woke up good and saw your text message, did you make it to your aunt's house yet?"

"I actually just pulled up, and it seems as if she's not home, I don't see her car anywhere."

"I hope you have a key to her house, if not, you're more than welcomed to come to my spot for a little while."

"As long as she didn't change the locks, my key should still work, but you're more than welcomed to come over, you can help me go through her pictures and hopefully we can find her old VCR in either her attic or basement."

"I'm going to shower, get dressed and I'll be right over."

"Can't wait to see you!"

Fifteen minutes later, Jay pulls up and calls me to let me know he's at the door.

"Hey handsome!" I greeted him with a big hug.

"Hey beautiful, it's good to finally see you," he greeted me with a hug and forehead kiss.

"You act like we don't video chat every night."

"That doesn't count, there's nothing better than seeing you in person."

"Aww, aren't you sweet."

"Yeah, yeah, now where do we start with your auntie's pictures?"

Jay and I pulled out two big storage bins that had photo albums, loose pictures, and VHS tapes.

# The Freak in Me

I was looking at old pictures of my aunt in her college years; she attended Elm City University, which is where her and my uncle met and I came across a photo album of my aunt and noticed that she had on a jacket that had Delta Pi Psi Sorority on it.

"Jay look at this picture and tell me you see what I'm seeing!"

"Yo, your aunt is a member of DPP? That's dope!! Y'all can connect on a totally different level now!"

Just then, my aunt and uncle walked in.

"There's my favorite niece!"
"Heyyyy!! I missed y'all so much!"

"We missed you more! Who is this handsome young man here?"

"So sorry, Auntie Chele and Uncle Brian, this is my friend JayVon, JayVon these are my parents as well as auntie and uncle, Chele and Brian."

# Saige the Gemini

"Nice to meet the both of you," Jay greeted my family.

"Nice to meet you too young man, are you staying for dinner?"

"Um, no, I don't want to impose on your time with Trice here."

"Jay, that was a rhetorical question, when my auntie asks if you're staying, she's basically telling you that you're staying and she's not taking no for an answer."

"Well then, I'd be more than happy to stay for dinner."

"What do we have here?" My auntie asked about all of her photos and tapes out on her living room floor.

"Oh, I was looking through your pictures, trying to see if I could find pictures or tapes of my biological parents, then I happened to stumble across this picture of you wearing a Delta Pi Psi jacket on, I didn't know you were in a sorority."

# The Freak in Me

"What do you know about Delta Pi Psi Sorority?"

I went to my suitcase and grabbed my line jacket, held it up and said, "This is what I know about Delta Pi Psi Sorority, and I'm now officially your sorority sister!"

"Wait!! Why didn't you tell me that you were pledging DPP? We would've flown up for your probate!"

"As soon as I get a date for the probate, I'll let you know."

"Wait, how did you get your line jacket already but didn't have your probate yet?" My uncle asked.

"Some of my prophytes decided to welcome me into the sorority before some of my other line sisters, they had one last private session that I had to complete in a certain time period, in which I crushed it, and they welcomed me right on the spot, I do have to go to the probate though and I would be honored for the both of you to be there."

Just as I said that, Jay cleared his throat and said, "Well damn, what about me?"

"You better be there, shit, you were there as my last mission, so it's only right that you're there to help me celebrate this new chapter in my life."

"Jay, are you in a fraternity?"

"Yes sir, I am, I'm a member of Beta Delta Mu Fraternity."

"Ahhh, now you're speaking my language."

"Are you in Beta Delta Mu?"

"I sure am."

"Nice to meet a fellow fraternity brother. Are the both of you originally from Connecticut?"

"Yea, born and raised, after college we moved out here to Georgia."

"That's what's up, I found out while I was pledging that my father and one of my uncles were also apart of BDM."

# The Freak in Me

"Nice, maybe one day we can get together and have lunch, I'd love to hear more about your BDM experience and see if I know your family who were Beta men."

"Most definitely."

"Trice, there are some tapes in one of these bins from my stepping days at ECU, and I think there are some photos of my sorority sistas and I doing community service events, and just hanging around campus."

For the next four hours Jay, my aunt, uncle and I went through pictures, watched VHS tapes and just talked about our initiation experiences it was so dope. Jay helped my aunt in the kitchen with dinner and as they were cooking, my uncle Brian and I got a chance to talk about my biological parents.

"Unc, do you know why my biological parents never wanted to reconnect with me?"

"I think they have their own demons they need to work through before they can reconnect with anyone in the family. They did and said a lot of fucked up things to people in the family and I think the embarrassment has gotten the best of them."

"What was it about me that they didn't want? Like what kind of parents conceive you and just dump you on family to raise?"

"Babygirl, you have to realize how blessed you are that your mother had enough sense to bring you to your aunt and I to raise as our own, she could've been one of those fucked parents to throw you into a trash can or some shit."

"I know unc, I just want to be able to sit and talk to them, I have no animosity towards them, I really just want a genuine relationship with them, I feel like a piece of me is still missing because I know nothing about them."

"I understand sweetheart, I do, have you talked to your grandparents lately? Maybe they can help you fill in some of those blanks that you have."

# The Freak in Me

"I haven't, maybe when I leave, I'll stay in New York for a few hours and go see them, talk to them and see if they can help me fill this void."

"I'm sure they'll be able to, and if they aren't, pray about your situation, pray and ask for your parents hearts to soften and for them to desire a relationship with you just as you do with them, you know they say prayer changes things.
"

"Thanks unc, I appreciate you and I know I don't say it as often as I should but I really do appreciate and love you and auntie Chele for taking me in as your own and keeping me even after you had children of your own."

"Did you think that after we had children of our own that we'd give you to someone else to raise?"

"Honestly, I did, I didn't know what to expect; I'm just glad I was able to be raised by family in a home where I was loved."

## Saige the Gemini

"We wouldn't have had it any other way," my aunt Chele said as she and Jay walked in with some hors d'oeuvres.

I excused myself to my old bedroom; my emotions were starting to get the best of me. Ten minutes later, Jay knocked on my bedroom door, "come on in."

"I came to check on you, your people were starting to get worried about you."

"I'll be alright, I just want to enjoy my time here, and then fly back to New York to see my grandparents, and try to get some answers from them regarding my mother and why she left me and doesn't want a relationship with me."

"I hate seeing you sad Trice, this makes my heart hurt, I can't imagine what you're going through right now."

"I feel like our situations are almost alike, in a way, I mean we both lost our parents, having to navigate this college life alone, not having our life givers around for some of our most important times of our lives."

"I can see that. You wanna get out of here for a little while and go sightseeing, skating or do something fun to get your mind off of things?"

"I would love that! I need to get my head together for my aunt's surprise party, let me go tell them I'll be gone for a while and we can be on our way."

Jay and I spent the next few hours sightseeing in Atlanta, we took so many pictures, it was ridiculous. I took in all of the history that was here in Atlanta, we also made plans on driving to Alabama before it was time for me to head back to Connecticut, Jay wanted to check out some properties down there for a business him and his frat brothers were starting.

# Saige the Gemini
## Auntie's Party

Jay and some of his frat brothers agreed to help me set up for my aunt's surprise party while my Uncle Brian made sure to keep her out of the house until I sent him the text that it was all right to make his way back home with Aunt Chele.

As the guests were starting to arrive, I was shocked to see my grandparents and they were shocked to see me as well, it was great to have my aunts, uncles, cousins, and grandparents here under one roof for a joyous occasion.

Around four o'clock I sent my uncle a text message letting him know that we were all set and that he could bring auntie home, the house was full of family and friends to help her celebrate her birthday. Jay and his brothers left just as Uncle Brian and Auntie Chele were pulling up.

Just as Uncle Brian and Auntie Chele were making their way up the driveway, a woman who looked like my auntie, just a little younger, was getting out of a car with a guy who I couldn't help but notice that looked like me.

When Aunt Chele stepped into the house everyone yelled "Surprise!" The look on her face was priceless, until she turned around and heard the mystery woman yell out, "Happy birthday big sis!"

My aunt rolled her eyes and ignored the woman; I then looked at the woman and said, "Ma?"

"Ma? I don't have any children so I can't be your mother."

I knew this woman was my mother and the guy with her was my father, now why they decided to disown me was still a mystery to me, but this wasn't the time or place to address either of them.

My aunt's face was so full of joy from seeing family and friends that she'd hadn't seen in a wile, she shed tears, had plenty of laughs, it

# Saige the Gemini

felt good to be able to do this for the woman who raised me as her own.

Three hours later all of the guests had left, the only people left were my grandparents and the woman and man who I knew were my parents.

"Trice, I'm about to bounce, I know you and your family have a lot to talk about."

"I appreciate everything you and your frat brothers did today, I owe y'all big time."

"You know I got you shorty, listen, if you need or want to talk later, hit me up."

"You know I will," I told him before making my way back into the house.

"Trice, how long are you going to be here?" My grandfather asked me.

"I'll be here until Sunday, I'm flying back to New York Sunday morning."

"How's school coming along?"

"School is great Big Mama, I'm acing all of my classes, just joined a sorority and I've already began making plans on the business I want to start when I graduate."

"That's good to hear, Lord willing, we'll be at your college graduation front and center, we are so proud of you Trice," my grandfather said.

"Thank you Pops, I appreciate you, Big Mama, Aunt Chele and Uncle Brian for everything you've done for me over the years, you all have been a true blessing to me."

"Insert the violin playing," said the mystery woman.

"Gina, cut your shit!" My grandfather yelled.

"Daddy, I'm just tired of all of this!"
I laughed at her then said, "Tired of all of what? Tired of being an absent parent? Tired of pretending that you don't have children? Tired of being the families fuck up?"

"Trice, calm down baby girl," my uncle said to me.

# Saige the Gemini

"Excuse my language Big Mama and Pops."

"Chris, are you ready to go? We should've never come here today."

"You damn right you shouldn't have! Let me tell the both of y'all something before you go, you did me a huge favor leaving me with auntie Chele and uncle Brian to raise, I don't know what demons the both of you are dealing with, but trust and believe when I tell you that you both better pray and ask for forgiveness because as of today, you are dead to me!"

My parents looked at me with a blank stare, then turned to my grandparents and said to them, "mama and daddy, we'll be seeing you when we get back to New York, we're going to leave today, there's nothing left here for us to celebrate."

My uncle Brian then said, "Gina and Christopher, I think the both of you and Trice need to go in the other room and have a heart to heart, y'all need to be open and honest about your issues and the real reason why you chose to give her to us to raise, this shit needs to stop and it needs to stop today, we are all grown and Trice deserves to know the truth and the three of you deserve to get to know one another."

"Uncle Brian, I'm not even in the mood today, I meant what I said, as of today they are dead to me, did you see how she really acted like she didn't know who I was and straight disowned me when she walked up in here? I'm good on them. Big Mama and Pops, I'm going to fly into New York on my way back home, I'll stop by and see you before driving to Connecticut," I told them before grabbing my phone and jacket and leaving the house.

As soon as I got into my car I called Jay, "what's up love?"

"I hope I'm not interrupting, if I am, just let me know."

"Nah, you're good love, are you alright?"

## Saige the Gemini

"Honestly? No I'm not alright, I just had a whole ass argument with my biological sperm donor and egg donor, I needed to get out of the house but then I realized I'm in Georgia and other than my family, you're the only other person I really know and trust down here."

"Damn ma, I'm sorry, I'm going to text you my address, come through, we'll talk when you get here."

"I'll see you shortly."

I got to Jay's house in like five minutes.

"Yo, you good?"

"Not in the least bit, do you have anything to drink, preferably something real strong."

"The bar is fully stocked, go help yourself to anything you want."

"Yo, why when my aunt and uncle were on their way into the house my biological sperm and egg donors showed up?"

"Seriously? Did y'all get a chance to talk?"

# The Freak in Me

"Peep this, I called Gina ma when I saw her, and she looked me dead in my eye and told me that she didn't have any children."

"Damn ma, I'm sorry to hear that, listen if you want to stay here tonight, we have more than enough rooms."

I walked over to where JayVon was sitting on the couch, I straddled him, and began kissing him, I needed and wanted to feel him on the inside of me.

Jay picked me up and brought me to his bedroom, laid me on his bed and kissed me deeply, both of his hand cupping my breasts. My hormones were going crazy; I wanted to fuck my frustrations away. Jay broke away from our kiss, took his shirt off, then took his shorts off, his dick was huge, and I wanted him to fill this pussy of mine up with every inch of it.

He put each of my legs up on his shoulders, and dove head first into my throbbing pussy and when I tell y'all his tongue felt heavenly, I mean just that.

"Jay, keep your tongue right there baby, ohmygawd! You're eating the fuck outta my pussy!"

He uttered no words, he looked at me with the most loving eyes, I knew the sex we were about to have was about to be more than just a fuck session, there was about to be some passion between us and I wasn't about to object to it. He slipped on a BDM XL condom and from the looks of it; his dick was still too big for it.

When he entered me, I gasped, I wasn't used to being with someone as large as him. "Jay, take it slow baby."

"I got you ma, let me know if I do anything that's uncomfortable to you."

He took it slow, each stroke was just the right tempo and once I got somewhat used to his length and width, I matched each stroke of his with a hip thrust of my own, we were in sync and it just felt right. Jay and I made love for almost two hours and for once in my life, I didn't feel empty inside when we were done.

"Jay, what are we doing? Or better yet, what did we just do?"

"I hope I helped you take your mind off of things for a while."

"What does this mean for us?"
"What do you want it to mean?"

"I'm not completely sure, but I do know I've never felt so connected to anyone else like I feel with you, somehow you make me feel safe and complete."

"Well listen, I'm here with you, we got a vibe going on, so I'm riding this wave with you until you get tired of me and tell me you no longer want to be bothered with me."

"I appreciate you, I really do. I need to figure all of this out, on top of the family drama I'm dealing with."

"When do you leave to head back home?"

## Saige the Gemini

"Sunday morning but I don't want to go back to my aunt and uncle's house and see her sister and brother-in-law again."

"Do you want to stay here? We have more than enough rooms and I'm sure my brother won't mind.

"That would be great, but I don't want to put you in the middle of my family drama."

"Nonsense, I told you I got you; let me get dressed and we can go get your things."

When we got to my aunt's house my grandparents were on their way to the airport and their youngest child and her husband were right behind them.

I introduced my grandparents to JayVon and they seemed to like him and I reminded my grandparents that I was going to fly into New York to spend some time with them before making my way back to campus in Connecticut. I then let my aunt and uncle know that I would be staying with Jay for the remainder of my stay in

# The Freak in Me

Georgia but I would make sure to see them before I left to head back home.

Jay and I grabbed something to eat before going back to his place; we put a movie on, Love Jones, ate, then somehow Jay's dick ended up in my mouth and before I knew it, I was riding him into ecstasy.

For the next two days while Jay went to class I spent time with my aunt and uncle.

"Trice, you still going through those pictures?"

"Aunt Chele, do you realize how many pictures you have? It's going to take me a while to get through all of them."

"I feel like you really only want to see pictures of my sorority sisters and me."

"You know me so well," I said laughing.

"They're in a photo album which is probably at the bottom of the bin."

I pulled three albums out, all pictures from my aunt's probate, her and her line sisters doing events after they graduated college. There were a few photos that stuck out to me; it was from a baby shower.

'Auntie, whose baby shower was this?"

She looked at the pictures then said, "Oh goodness, I totally forgot about this, this was a baby shower for one of my line sisters, Yvette, she got pregnant during our senior year of college, her daughter should be around the same age as you. What was her daughter's name?"

As I looked through the photos, the woman who had the baby looks so familiar, she reminds me of someone I know.

"Auntie, do you still keep in contact with your line sisters?"

"Of course I do, most of them remember you when you first started living with us, they still ask about you and everything."

"That's dope, I think I'll be throwing a baby shower soon too for..."

# The Freak in Me

"Trice, you better not tell me you're pregnant."

"Hell no auntie, I need to hit millionaire status before I let anyone knock me up."

"Well who's the shower for?"

"One of my line sisters, Akira Delaney."

"Delaney? That's my line sister Yvette's last name."

"That's it!!"

"What's it?"

"I knew she looked familiar, but I know I didn't know her, she's got to be my friend Akira's mother."

"Do her parents know she's pregnant?"

"Nope, she's scared to tell them, her father is a pastor and she's not ready for what he may say or think about her being pregnant out of wedlock."

"Yvette married a guy who said he's always knew he was going to be a pastor. Text your friend and ask her what her parents names are."

"I'm going to text her this picture and ask if that's her mother."

As I was waiting for Akira to respond, Jay sent me a text asking where I was. I let him know I was at my aunt's house and invited him over. Just as I was letting Jay in the house, Akira called me.

"What's up girlie?"

"Yo! Talk about a throwback picture of my mother! But, where did you get it from?"

"That's your mother for real? Auntie, you won't believe this, my line sister is your line sisters daughter."

"Line sister? My mother isn't in a sorority Trice."

"How sure are you about that? From these pictures I'm looking at, you r mother and my aunt crossed together."

"Trice, let me call you back."

# The Freak in Me

"So Yvette's daughter is pledging Delta Pi Psi too?"

"Yea, but she has to sit out for a while until she has the baby."

"I'm going to pray for her, because from what I remembered about her father, he was a no nonsense type of guy."

My uncle startled us when he interjected. "Who's a no nonsense guy?"

"Remember my line sister Yvette? Her husband."

"Robert Delaney?"

"Is that her husbands name?"

"Yea, he crossed into Beta Delta Mu a year after me."

"Wait, Akira's pops is a member of Beta Delta Mu?" Jay asked looking perplexed.

"Yea, if it's the same Robert Delaney I'm thinking about, he crossed a year after I did but he hasn't been active since about a year or two after he crossed, he doesn't even come to our Founder's Day celebrations."

"It doesn't make any sense though, he's so against fraternities and sororities according to Akira, but yet he's a member of the most erotic fraternity around," I said.

"Maybe he stepped aside when he became a pastor and doesn't want anyone to knowing that side of him," Jay responded.

"That might be it, but I think it's super contradicting."

"Welp, my mind is blown," Jay said then asked, "Mr. Brian, do you happen to have a picture of him by any chance?"

Uncle Brian went to his bedroom and returned with a small photo album. He opened it and right there was a picture of him and his line brothers and their neos.

"Yo, that's Akira's father right there!" Jay said pointing to one of the guys in the photo.

# The Freak in Me

"This is funny but crazy at the same time," I said.

"This guy is a nutcase, he's constantly on my brother's case about joining a fraternity and Akira, in my opinion wants to join a sorority but she won't 'cause of her father; wait until I tell my brother this shit."

I sat quietly; I knew Akira knew nothing about her father being a member of Beta Delta Mu but I also knew I wasn't going to be the one to tell her either, I already spilled the beans to her about her mother being in a sorority, I didn't even tell her it was Delta Pi Psi.

"Jay, you can't say anything to Justice about Akira's father, 'cause if he says something to her, she's going to want to know how he found out and when they put two and two together, they'll both know we've been dealing with one another and then Akira will know that I know her father is in BDM and that's not a conversation I want to have with her, especially since I just told her that her mother is in a sorority."

"I got you Ma, neither one of them will hear it from me."

"Thank you, I appreciate it."
"No doubt."

"Are y'all hungry? Brian and I are about to cook."

"You know we are auntie, please make enough so I can make a plate to bring with me to the airport."

"You know I always overcook so there will be plenty, as well as desserts for you to take back as well."

"You're the best!"
While Uncle Brian and Aunt Chele went to start dinner, Jay and I went to my old room to talk.

"Trice, I need to tell you something."
The seriousness in Jay's voice made me nervous.

"You're making me nervous, what's up?"

# The Freak in Me

"It's nothing bad, I really don't even want to admit this to you."

"Don't want to admit what?"
The first thing that came to mind was that he had a girlfriend somewhere and I was merely his sidepiece.

"I'm beginning to fall for you and hard."
There was no denying that I was beginning to fall for him too, but I needed to make sure Xavier and I were done for good and I needed Jay to make sure he wasn't craving other women, I mean let's be real, we're still in college and he lives in Georgia and I'm in Connecticut.

"Quiet as it's kept, I'm beginning to fall hard for you too."

"So what are we going to do about it?"

"I'm not sure, I mean we live in different states, we're still in college and let's be honest, there's temptation all around us, I think we should let things play out on their own and see what happens."

# Saige the Gemini

"Fair enough, question for you."

"Answer for you."

"Are we keeping this thing between us under wraps?"

"I would like to, I'm a private person for the most part and who or what I'm doing is no one's business but me and that person's."

"Definitely feel you on that."
"Are you okay with us being under wraps?"

"Yea, seeing as though we're not exclusive, I have no problem with it."

"Thank you for being understanding."

"I told you I got you Ma," he said before walking over to me and kissing me.

What started out as a little peck quickly turned into much more and before I knew it, Jay was standing behind me, my sweatpants were around my ankles and he was entering me from behind.

"FUCK Trice, you're wet as hell."
"It's all your fault, but keep your voice down."

# The Freak in Me

"FUCK!!"

"Jay, you're about to make me cum!!"

"Let's cum together."

"You gotta pull out baby."

"Hell no."

"I can't stand…ahhhh!" I couldn't get the rest of my sentence out before the orgasm ripped through my body.

Jay and I climaxed together and I was sure my aunt and uncle heard us, keeping quiet wasn't one of our strengths.

We went to the bathroom that was connected to my room to get cleaned up for dinner.

"When we returned downstairs the first thing my aunt and uncle did was start laughing.

"What's so funny?"

"The two of you, y'all are cute together and by the sounds of it, y'all enjoy each other immensely."

# Saige the Gemini

"We're sorry, I take full accountability for our actions," Jay said to them.

"Nonsense, we were younger once, we know how the spur of the moment fuck sessions can be."

""Quiet as it's kept, we still get those spur of the moment fuck sessions in," my uncle said winking at me aunt.

"T.M.I. uncle Brian," I told him laughing. I then said, "We meant no disrespect, Aunt Chele and Uncle Brian."

"We know, we're not tripping, you're grown and this young man seems as if he has some real feelings for you, so no harm, no foul, as long as y'all are being safe and responsible, we're good."

"We are," Jay and I said simultaneously.

For the next three hours my aunt, uncle, Jay and myself sat around the table eating, talking about school and sorority and fraternity life.

# The Freak in Me

"Trice, when are you going to see Big Mama and Pops?"

"I leave out tomorrow around eleven so once I get my car I'm going to see them and talk to them to see if they can shed some light on that sister and brother-in-law of yours."

"When you get there, keep an open mind, there's a lot you're going to have to unpack and remember, Gina and Christopher were young when they had you so show them a little bit of grace 'cause they did the right thing by having us raise you," Aunt Chele said tearing up.

"I will auntie, or I'll say I'll try to keep an open mind, but that crap they pulled at your birthday party really left a bad taste in my mouth."

"We know it did, there's a lot you still have to learn and figure out about those two, and I'd be lying if I said it was going to be easy," Uncle Brian told me.

# Saige the Gemini

"Aunt Chele, Uncle Brian, I appreciate y'all, I really do; I'm going to come over in the morning before I head to the airport."

"Alright sweetie, y'all get back to your destination safely, call or text us to let us know you made it in safely. Jay, take our numbers, you've broken bread with us and we can tell that our niece is very fond of you so that makes you family," Aunt Chele said as she was writing her and Uncle Brian's numbers down for JayVon.

"Thank you both for welcoming me into your home with open arms, it has been a pleasure meeting the both of you."

"The pleasure was all ours."
"Jay, do you by any chance golf?"

"Not really, I've always wanted to learn but no one I know golfs."

"Well, now you know someone who will teach you. If you're not busy next weekend we can go to a golf course if you're up for it."

"Most definitely!"

# The Freak in Me

Jay and I made our way back to his place and thankfully Justice wasn't around. I'd done a great job dodging him while I was staying there. I didn't want him going back to Akira telling her that we met and her insecurities going through the roof. I honestly didn't even want her knowing that JayVon and I knew one another or even sleeping together.

# Saige the Gemini
## The Next Morning...

Jay cooked us breakfast, we ate, showered together, had a passion session in the shower of course and I finished packing my suitcase.

"Trice, I'm going to come visit you within the next month or so."

"Okay, let me know a few days in advance so I can get us a room and make sure my schedule is clear."

"No need for a room, my parents house is not too far from you, that's where Justice and I stay when we're back home."

"Bet; you know I'm going to miss you, right?"

"I'm going to miss you too, do me a favor please."

"What's up?"

"Keep her wet and tight for me."

# The Freak in Me

I laughed then said, "you're funny, but you know she stays wet and tight."

"You bout to have me take you again," he told me stroking his already rock hard dick.

"Nope, you're going to make late and miss my flight, and I still have to go see my aunt and uncle before I drop the rental off."

If you say so shorty, I'm going to have to take a cold shower after you leave."

"Take a pic and send it to me, please and thank you."

"Only you," he said laughing.
He brought my suitcase to my car for me, we had a long hug, passionate kiss and we said our see ya laters. I stopped by to see my aunt and uncle before making my way to the airport, we talked some more, took some pictures like we always did when we were together. My aunt made me two plates to bring with me; we said our see you laters and I was on my way to the rental terminal to return the car then headed to the airport.

# Saige the Gemini

I sent Jay a text to let him know I was about to board the plane, and sent him another when I finally landed and arrived to my car safely; he told me to hit him when I made it to my grandparents house so he'd know I was good.

The argument my biological egg and sperm donor had was just the tip of the iceberg; there were some skeletons or generational curses or trauma that needed to be talked about worked through and deaded sooner rather than later.

When I pulled up to my grandparents house my biological egg and sperm donors were sitting on the porch trying to figure out who I was in the car behind the tinted windows.

"Breathe Trice, be calm, stay cool, don't let them anger you or take you out of character," I said aloud to myself.

I stepped out of the car, fixed my outfit, stretched real quick and made my way up the stairs to my grandparent's porch.

# The Freak in Me

"Damn I go to Georgia to see my sister, you're there, I come back home to spend some time with my parents and here you are again, you got a tracker on me or something?"

"Gina, you're not that important to me for me to track you. I came here to see my grandparents before I to back to campus; you're not relevant to me right now."

"Have some respect for your elders young lady, we're still your parents," Christopher said to me standing up.

I laughed hysterically then said, "parents? According to y'all not too long ago y'all don't have any children, isn't that what you said?" As far as I'm concerned Auntie Chele and Uncle Brian are my parents, you and Gina are my donors, nothing more but maybe a lot less."

I walked right past them, walked into my grandparent's house and greeted them, "Hey Pops and Big Mama! How are y'all doing?"

# Saige the Gemini

"We woke up this morning so we have no reason to complain, how are you baby girl?" My grandfather responded.

"I'm good Pops, just saw your daughter and son-in-law as I was coming in."

"How'd that go?" my grandmother asked.

"How do you think? For some reason Gina thinks I'm stalking her and all of a sudden now Chris wants to claim himself and Gina as my parents, but I'm not paying them any mind. I came to spend time with the both of you before heading back to school."

"Trice, what's your major?"
"Business administration with a minor in communications and marketing."

"That's my girl, listen, I have to run out for a little while so I'll let you ladies have some time to talk amongst yourselves," my grandfather said before kissing me on my forehead and leaving.

"Trice have you ever thought about pledging a sorority?"

# The Freak in Me

I was a little hesitant to tell her that I was in Delta Pi Psi, but I ripped the band-aid off and just told her, "I'm actually a newly crossed member of Delta Pi Psi Sorority."

My grandmother just stared at me, then she began laughing, once she gathered herself, she said, "This shit must run in the family. Trice, you were born into a family who love sex, you know Chele, Gina and I are all members of DPP."

"Wait, what?!"
My grandmother couldn't contain her laughter; she was laughing so hard that she had tears coming out of her eyes.

"I just found out auntie Chele was a member, I was going through all of her pictures when I got to her house, and saw her with some of her line sisters. I never knew Gina went to college let alone joined a sorority, and you're a member too?"

My grandmother got up from her chair then said, "Follow me."

# Saige the Gemini

We went into her back bedroom that for as long as I could remember was used for storage instead of a guest bedroom. In one of the closets was a storage chest, I pulled it out for her and placed it on top of one of the tables. The key she kept around her wrist opened the chest and in it was a mixture of Delta Pi Psi paraphernalia as well as Beta Delta Mu paraphernalia.

"Wait, Pops is in Beta Delta Mu?"
"He sure is, I told you that you come from a family who loves sex and I meant it."

"Mind blown," was all I managed to say, my family was so dope, never in a million years would I have thought my family would be a bunch of sex lovers on the level of being members of Delta Pi Psi and Beta Delta Mu."

I reached for my phone to text JayVon to tell him the new I just found out only to realize I had left my phone in my car. "I'll be right back grandma, I forgot my phone in the car."

# The Freak in Me

"Okay, I'm going to go through this stuff and see if I can find my pictures from my college says with my sorority sisters."

I ran to my car, grabbed my phone and noticed I had missed phone calls and text messages from Jay, Xavier, Akira and Soror ATM.

"What the hell is going on at ECU?" I hit Jay back first, "Damn, it's about time, I was about to assemble a search team to find you, is everything okay?"

"Yeah, I just realized I forgot my phone in the car, I'm good though."

"How are your grandparents?" "They're good, yo! Why did I just find out that my grandparents are in DPP and BDM?"

"Really? No wonder your ass is a little freak that shit is in your bloodline for real."

I shook my head and laughed, "here's the kicker, Gina, my biological egg donor is also a member of DPP, my grandmother just told me."

# Saige the Gemini

"Do you think if you bring it up to her it'll be a way you can start forming a bond with her?"

"After the way her and her husband greeted me when I pulled up to my grandparents house earlier, I highly doubt it and if I'm being honest with myself, I'm done trying to have a relationship with her and her husband. I promise you, there's something with them and it's going to take a lot longer than the time I have now to figure it out and work through it with them."

"I feel you, hit me if you need to talk, I don't to want to keep you from your family."

"Alright love, I'll call you tonight."
Instead of calling Xavier back I opted to send him a text message. *"Hey X, I noticed I missed your call, what's up?"*
While I waited for him to text me back, I called Akira back, "What's up sis?"

"Where the hell have you been? I know you've heard about the drama within DPP between ATM and SIYF."

# The Freak in Me

"Hell no I haven't heard, I've been in Georgia with my family, right now I'm in New York visiting my grandparents, I'm oblivious to everything going on at ECU."

"Well listen, when you get back on the road, hit me up."

"Okay mama."

Lastly I called Soror ATM back, "Bitch where the fuck have you been?"

"Georgia with my family, what's up? I heard things amongst the sorors at ECU are crazy right now."

"Trice, how come you didn't tell me you're related to Soror Smut Me Out?"

"I don't even know who that is," I told her genuinely confused.

"I just sent you a picture, check your messages."

I looked at my messages and there was a picture of Gina whose sorority name was Smut Me Out.

# Saige the Gemini

"ATM, I legit just found out like ten minutes ago that she was even in the sorority, she's my biological egg donor but she didn't raise me, shit, to be real she doesn't even claim me as her child."

"FUCK!!" was all I heard from ATM, then dead silence.

"What the hell is the issue with her?" "When are you coming back to campus? This is a conversation we'll have to have in person."

I'll be back either tonight or tomorrow morning."

"Hit me as soon as you get back and get settled in."

"Most definitely."
"This woman better not have messed up my chances of staying in Delta Pi Psi," I said to myself.

I sent a text to JayVon, *"I'm about to book a one way flight to Georgia and transfer to AU with you."*

# The Freak in Me

I placed my phone in my back pocket before heading back into the house. My grandmother was still in the back room going through all of her college stuff.

"You alright baby?"

"Yes and no grandma."

"What's going on?"

"I think Gina might've unknowingly screed me over with the sorority."

"How?"

"I'm not sure yet, one of my big sisters called me asking me why I didn't tell her I was legacy and related to Soror Smut Me Out."

"Do you need me to make a few phone calls so you won't have any issues with the sorority?"

"If you could, that would be great Big Mama."

"You know I'd do anything for you, don't worry about whatever mess Gina had or has going on, she's a legacy because of me and so are you, I'm not going to let her fuck up our families legacy, daughter or not."

"This is why you're my favorite Big Mama, you've always had my back."

"And I'll continue to until I take my last breath. What are your plans after college Trice?"

"I really want to open a swingers club with my line sisters."

"Oh, you're taking this DPP thing to the next level, well you know me and your grandfather, as well as Chele and Brian will be here for you if you need anything."

"I know Big Mama and I promise to make all of you proud of me and my accomplishments."

"You already have, just keep doing well in school, get that degree, open that club, have a special section for the fifty and up crew cause you know we still like to get our freak on every once in a while," Big Mama told me with a wink of the eye.

# The Freak in Me

"TMI Big Mama, entirely TMI!!"

She looked at me, shook her head and laughed.

Once I finally got settled back in my dorm room, showered, made myself something to eat, I sent Soror ATM a text to let her know that I was back on campus and that she and Soror SIYF could come through whenever they were available, five minutes later, there was a knock on my door.

"Come in!"

"Trice, or should I say Soror Porn Star," Soror SIYF greeted me with much attitude.

"Good evening ladies."

Soror ATM then said, "Trice, I want to apologize for the conversation we had yesterday regarding Soror Smut Me Out, I didn't realize the both of you didn't have a relationship with one another."

"It's not a problem, it's probably for the best."

# The Freak in Me

Soror SIYF rolled her eyes at me after my last statement, I don't know what her issue is but I'm not it.

"Is there any issued between us Soror Squirt In Ya Face?"

"Issue, no, there's no issue other than the fact that you're my younger sister."

"Wait, what? Younger sister?" SIYF replied, "yeah, as soon as I saw you at the informational I knew we had to be related, then I started doing some digging and found this," she showed me a picture of her, Gina, Christopher and a baby that I could only assume was me, looked like I was only a few days old.

I looked at the both of them puzzled as hell; my life seemed to get more complicated as the days passed.

"This shit doesn't make any sense, who were you raised by?"

"Christopher's family."

# Saige the Gemini

"Why did I not know I had an older sister? Why does it seem as if you have an attitude with me though?"

"My issue isn't with you Trice, it's with Gina and Christopher, they had me knowing damn well they weren't ready to have children, then three months later, they were pregnant with you. There was some sort of family blow up with Gina, Chele, and Big Mama. Aunt Chele wanted Gina to leave the both of us with her and Uncle Brian but Gina and Christopher's dumb asses refused for some reason and Christopher's parents ended up agreeing to take me in because the only other option was for me to go into foster care because none of our other aunts or uncles were ready to be instant parents."

"This is crazy, I wish I would've known before I left to go to Georgia, I would've had you come with me to the surprise party I had for Aunt Chele.

# The Freak in Me

"I thought about going to see her for her birthday but I didn't want to bring drama to the party cause my intentions would have been to confront both Gina and Chris."

"We're definitely related cause I damn sure read them the riot act after the party, then again when I went to New York to see Big Mama and Pops."

"How are Pops and Big Mama doing?"

"They are well, Soror ATM, do you mind if my sister and I have a moment to ourselves?"

"Not a problem, I know y'all have a lot to discuss."

"So, you know Gina, Aunt Chele and Big Mama are all in Delta Pi Psi, right?"

"I found out about Gina about ten minutes before Kat called you, I ain't even know that trifling bitch went to college, but Aunt Chele and Big Mama, this is the first time I'm hearing about them being in DPP, we come from a family of freaks don't we?"

# Saige the Gemini

"Yo! I said the same thing to Big Mama; we should go see her and Pops together one weekend, I'm sure they would love to see you."

"Let me know when you want to go and I'll make myself available."

"Bet, let's exchange numbers, we have a lot to catch up on."

## Four Hours Later...

I was lying down and all of a sudden there were loud knocks on my door. "Whoever is banging on my door better be bleeding or about to go into labor!"

I got up to open my door and lo and behold it was Xavier.

"X, what the fuck are you banging on my door like that for?"

"You haven't been answering any of my calls or returning any of my text messages and I haven't seen you in a while so I came over to make sure you were alright."

# The Freak in Me

"Yo, first of all, I'm not obligated to answer any of your phone calls or text messages, second of all, the last message I got from you, I replied and never heard anything back, so that's on you."

"Where the fuck have you been?"
"Minding the business that pays me."

"Always gotta have a smart ass comment."

"Listen, you came to my room uninvited, you can leave if you don't like my smart ass mouth."

"You know what, fuck you Trice."
I started laughing, "You miss this pussy, don't you?"

"Honestly, hell yea and I miss you, do you miss me?"

"Not at all."
"Damn, you didn't have to respond so quickly."

"I wasn't trying to spare your feelings, just being honest with you. Is there anything else I can help you with?"

# Saige the Gemini

"Wow, I clearly caught you on a bad day, I'll leave, but maybe one day this coming weekend we can go out to eat and talk; I meant it when I said that I missed you and I want to have an open and honest talk with you about our future."

"I'll hit you when I'm available and we can go from there."

"Okay and I apologize if I disturbed you."

"Yup."

Just as I was about to lay back down there was another knock on my door, "It's open," I said to whomever was on the other side.

"Well damn trick where the hell you been? You've been M.I.A. for a minute," Jade said as her and the other ladies came in.

"I done been to Georgia then to New York to handle some family business; what's up with y'all?"

"Nothing much, we thought since Akira decided to drop the line you followed suit, you've missed a lot of the most recent initiation meet-ups."

"Nah, I haven't dropped off line, just had to go handle some business."

Kyra then said, "Do you know why Akira dropped off line?"

"Kinda, but that's something you'll have to talk to her about."

The ladies looked at each other, then they all looked at me like they knew I was hiding a secret for Akira, which I was.

"Anyway, have we gotten a date for probate yet? I know it should be coming up soon."

"You think the big sisters will let you cross since you've missed like four of the meet-ups?" Kiera asked.

"I hope they will, I'm sure I'll be getting a phone call or text from one of them soon to talk, I'll figure it out from there."

"Bet, well let us know what they say, we were supposed to cross as the Sensual Six, it would suck if it were only the Fornicating Four," Kiera said.

"What y'all got planned tonight? I have something I want to run by you."

"We don't have anything planned," Kyra responded.

"Bet, whose room are we meeting in?"

"We can meet in mine," Marie offered.

"Great, let me shower real quick, can one of y'all call Akira and let her know we're meeting in Marie's room? I'll be over there in about twenty minutes."

"You sound like you're about to do a whole PowerPoint presentation or something," Marie said laughing.

"Something like that," I told her then winked.

# The Freak in Me

"I sent a text to Akira, she said she'd meet us at Marie's room in fifteen minutes," Kyra told us.

"Bet, I'm about to hop in the shower real quick then I'll be right over there."

## Half Hour Later

"Okay ladies, I'm not going to keep you too long but there's a business idea I've had on my heart and mind since our first meeting with the ladies of Delta Pi Psi and I think if the six of us pull our resources together after graduation, this can be a very profitable business venture for us and we can possibly be millionaires before we hit our thirties if we do this right."

"Well, you had my attention when you said we could be millionaires before we turn thirty," Marie said.

"So being that we're about to cross into Delta Pi Psi Sorority, I think we should take this experience and turn it into something major. What do you ladies think about opening up a swingers club along with an adult movie theater and toy line?"

Akira immediately began shaking her head no and rolling her eyes.

"Hell no, I can't have my name attached to some shit like that, my parents would definitely disown me if I was apart of anything like that."

"You're really bugged out Akira, you're trying to cross into a sorority whose whole initiation process is centered around sex, but yet you're cringing over being part owner of a business that's going to make you a millionaire in a couple of years? Make it make sense to me please, cause I really want to understand," Kiera said obviously irritated with Akira.

"Kiera, don't start with me today, I'm not in the mood for your shit. I said what I said and I'm not explaining shit to you."

# The Freak in Me

"Okay ladies, this is supposed to be a no-judgment zone, those who want to be apart of this business venture will not judge those who choose not to be apart of it, we are sisters so chill with the back and forth, please and thank you."

"Trice, please continue explaining this business venture."

For the next half hour my girls and I talked about the possibility of going into business together.

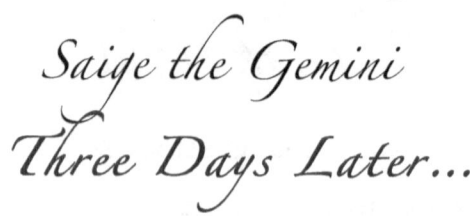

# Saige the Gemini
## Three Days Later...

I left my communications class and was on my way back to my room when I happened to see Soror Squirt In Ya Face.

"Sis, what's good with ya?"
"Nothing much, just left my last class for the week, what's going on with you?"

"Nothing really, does your offer still stand to go see Big Mama and Pops?"

"Hell yea, it's an open invitation."
"Are you free this weekend?"

"Sure am, we can leave tonight if you'd like that way we can have the extra day with them."

"I'm cool with that, let me go pack a bag, let the other sorors know I'll be unavailable for the remainder of the week and I'll meet you at your room."

Laniyah met me at my room just as I had finished packing, I had my music going and I didn't hear her when she knocked before pushing the door open to let herself in.

"Girl, you startled the hell out of me!"

"My bad, I thought I knocked loud enough over the music so you could hear me."

"It's all good, you all ready to get on the road?"

"Hell yea, it's been too long since I've seen this side of the family, it'll be great to see Big Mama and Pops."

"If I would've thought about it earlier, I would have seen if Aunt Chele and Uncle Brian could have taken a weekend trip, we could've all been under the same roof this weekend for a real family reunion."

"There will be other times, when we can all be together, I really just want to see Big Mama and Pops, and thank them for everything."

"I feel you, let's bounce and get on the road, hopefully 15 isn't a shit show and traffic will be light."

# Saige the Gemini

"I'm ready."

Laniyah and I made our way to my car without any of my girls seeing us, the last thing I needed was them asking why the two of us were together and with bags at that.

We breezed down the Merritt Parkway, thankfully there was no traffic, and we made it to our grandparent's house in about an hour and ten minutes.

"You've gotta be shittin' me," Laniyah said as we pulled up to the house.

"What's wrong?"

Before she answered, I had answered my own question; our biological egg and sperm donor were on the porch about to walk into the house.

"Remember, we're here to see Big Mama and Pops, ignore those two."

"It's going to be hard, but okay."

I rang the doorbell cause I knew my grandfather would answer the door, once we heard him coming I hid on the side of the porch so Laniyah would be the first person he saw when he opened the door.

"Oh my Lord!! Are my eyes playing tricks on me?"

"Hey Pops! How are you?"
"Babygirl, I'm better now, come on in this house!"

"Well, what am I? Chopped liver?" I asked teasing.

"You could never be," my grandfather replied.

My grandmother came into the living room and instantly began crying when she saw Laniyah standing there.

"Oh my word," was all she could say.

Seeing my grandmother cry made me start crying, and then Laniyah began crying.

"What's going on in here?" Gina said walking into the living room. As soon as she saw Laniyah and I in the living room, the glass of water she was holding was suddenly on the floor in a million pieces.

"What the hell are y'all doing here?" She asked.

"It's nice to see you too Gina," I said sarcastically.

She rolled her eyes then said, "Trice and Laniyah, it's so nice to see the both of you."

"You can stop lying, you know you aren't happy to see either of us," Laniyah said to her.

"Listen, regardless of anything, I'm still your mother and you will respect me," Gina said looking at the both of us.

I started laughing, it wasn't intentional but this lady had lost her everlasting mind.

"Something funny Trice?"

"Nothing, wait, I lied, you're funny. A week ago you denied me to my face told me you didn't have any children, now you're our mother and you want us to respect you? That's just crazy to me, that's all."

# The Freak in Me

"Okay now, everyone sit down, it's time to talk and get this mess between the four of you out in the open and healing to begin," Big Mama said to all of us.

"Christopher, get your ass out here now," my grandfather yelled.

Christopher came from one of the back rooms and sat next to Gina and Laniyah and I sat next to one another on the love seat.

Big Mama began, "Gina and Christopher, you owe it to your daughters to tell them the truth as to why y'all gave them to family to raise."

"Mama, I really don't want to do this right now."

"I don't think she asked you if you wanted to do it right now," my grandfather told her.

"Alright, fine," Gina said while rolling her eyes.

Tears began filling Gina's eyes; this was the first time seeing her show some type of vulnerability. Christopher was sitting next to her looking like he was about to be exposed for some foul shit; this was about to be interesting.

"Okay Laniyah and Trice, I've been a fucked up individual for a long ass time, it almost feels as if with anything and everything I do, it's never enough. I used to run away from home like every other week, and not because my parents were terrible to me or anything but because I wanted the freedom I saw my sister Chele have, not thinking about the fact that Chele is almost ten years older than me. Well, on one of my excursions away from home, Christopher and I met and at the time, I was only about eight years old and Christopher was fifteen."

Christopher then interjected, "I was messed up as well, young and at that time, I didn't know that messing with someone seven years younger than me was a crime, I had no real guidance."

"I guess I got it honest then," Laniyah said.

# The Freak in Me

"My parents were around but they were at their wits end between them doing drugs, no steady jobs and raising my brother and I."

Gina then said, "Long stories short, when I was thirteen, we got pregnant with Laniyah, then three months later, we got pregnant with you Trice. We knew nothing about being parents, so when we found out we were pregnant with you Trice, we decided it would be best to have Laniyah to be raised by your father's parents because by that time they had somewhat cleaned up their act they had well paying jobs and they were able to better provide than we could."

Christopher continued, "Trice, when we had you, Chele and Brian were still newlyweds and trying for a baby of their own and by that time, they'd graduated from college and were doing damn good for themselves, so your grandparents, Chele and Brian, your mother and I all decided it would be in your best interest to be raised by Chele and Brian as they could provide you with the stability you needed."

"So why did y'all decide to stay away for so long? Why didn't you tell me when I was Aunt Chele's for her birthday that I had an older sister?" I asked genuinely confused.

"Trice, we still have a lot of healing to do and that's from the inside out."

"Wow," seemed to be the only word Laniyah could say before she stood up and headed to the front door.

"Laniyah, please don't leave," Gina said tearfully.

"I'm not leaving, I just need to step outside, digest all of this and get some fresh air."

"Gina, can I talk to you privately for a minute?"

"Trice, you can call me mom, you don't have to call me Gina."

"You've never been a mother to me so why would I start calling you mom now?"

# The Freak in Me

"It's a respect thing," Christopher said.

"Respect is a two way street, you gotta give it to get it," I told him.

Gina and I walked to the back deck; we stared at each other intensely for a good three minutes before she broke the silence and said, "What was so private that we couldn't talk about it in front of everyone else?"

"Delta Pi Psi. How'd you get in and does your husband know about it?"

"How'd you know I'm in Delta Pi Psi?"

"Cause I'm in it too and the last time I was here I got a phone call about a video of you in some compromising positions with some men of Beta Delta Mu and DPP threatened to kick Laniyah and I out because of your shit on some guilty by association mess."

"FUCK!" she yelled, then said, "Christopher doesn't know I'm in the sorority, he doesn't even know that I graduated from college with a psychology degree."

# Saige the Gemini

My eyes widened, she was smarter than I gave her credit for.

"Wait, a bachelor's in psychology? Seriously?"

"Yea, there a was period of time when he and I weren't seeing eye to eye, we both got our GEDs at the same time, and he seemed to be content with that. I on the other hand knew that I wanted more, for myself as well as for you and your sister; it was never my intent on giving y'all up and not coming back to get y'all so we can live like a regular family. I've always wanted us under one roof but Chris on the other hand has been fine with letting you girls stay with family so we could live carefree."

"So, what's really good with you and this alleged video with guys from BDM?"

"The videos are real, during the time Chris and I took a break from one another is when I enrolled in college, which is quite naturally where I found out about Delta Pi Psi. Well, I was, back

# The Freak in Me

then, very desperate to be apart of a sisterhood so I pretty much did anything and everything my big sisters told me or dared me to do, one of which was being in a gangbang with a bunch of the guys from BDM and if you've encountered any old school guys from BDM, they're really freaky and they like to hang thinks over your head and according to some of them, that video of me with almost twenty of them is what they have over me."

"Damn," was all I could say; then I asked, "are you sure your husband doesn't know about any of this?"

"I'm about fifty percent sure."
"Big Mama can't do anything about the video? She's the one that saved Laniyah and I from getting kicked out."

"She knows nothing about the video as far as I know and honestly, that's not something I'm completely comfortable talking to her about."

# Saige the Gemini

"Swallow your pride and get it done, This is something that can not only affect you, but it can also affect Aunt Chele, Laniyah and me and I've worked too damn hard to get into Delta Pi Psi on my own to allow some shit from your past to fuck me up."

"I'll talk to her about it tomorrow and see what she says. Trice, I want to sincerely apologize for any hurt or pain I have caused you over the years, I know Chele and Brian always told you that they were your aunt and uncle instead of your parents and I know I can never make up for all the time we've been apart, but I'd like to hopefully start to cultivate a relationship with you, if you're up to it."

"We can do that, but I'm going to have to find me a therapist and I really think the four of us need to go to family therapy, y'all really did a number on Laniyah more so than me."

"I'm okay with going to therapy, I think it'll be good for us."

# The Freak in Me

As Gina and I were walking back to the living room, we heard Laniyah and Christopher arguing loudly.

"What is going on in here?" Gina asked standing in the middle of the both of them.

"Your oldest daughter thinks she's grown, that's the problem, and she doesn't think she needs to respect me as her father."

"Listen any male with a dick and sperm can make a baby, but a real man takes car of his responsibilities, like raising his children instead of making them go live with family that doesn't give a damn about them."

"Laniyah, what happened?" Big Mama asked.

"What didn't happen? Anything and everything, and Chris, I bet you don't even know that I remember seeing and watching you having sex with multiple women when you and Gina took a break, do you?"

"Wait, what?" we all said at the same time.

# Saige the Gemini

"Oh yea, Gina and Christopher took a break from one another and he ended up going back to his parents house so he could figure life out and during that time, he was banging a bunch of different women, sometime two or three of them at the same time and this nasty bastard didn't have the common courtesy or sense to not fuck them in the very room I slept in; so I guess this is why I'm as sexually active and free as I am, and he can't handle it."

"What I can't handle is the fact that my oldest daughter is a slut just like her mother."

Before I realized it, I had punched Christopher dead in his face; it wasn't our fault that we had fucked up parents. Pops drew his pistol with the quickness; one thing he didn't play about was his daughters and granddaughters.

"Christopher, I think it's time for you to excuse yourself from my house," my grandfather told him.

# The Freak in Me

"Mr. Pennington, I didn't mean to disrespect you, your house or granddaughters in any way, Laniyah, please forgive me."

Laniyah rolled her eyes at him and made her way up the stairs.

Pops replied, "I understand, but for the peace of my family, I think you need to separate yourself for a while, let me talk to my girls, cool things down and when it's cool for you to come back, I'll give you a call."

"Fair enough Mr. Pennington, and again, I apologize for my outburst."

Christopher excused himself from the house. Gina went upstairs to talk to Laniyah, so Pops, Big Mama and I began talking.

"Trice, did you and Gina have a productive talk?" Big Mama asked.

"Yea, we talked, she said she was willing to work on our relationship as well as start therapy, so we'll see."

# Saige the Gemini

"Good, y'all all need therapy and what the fuck did Christopher mean when he called Laniyah and Gina sluts?"

I looked at Big Mama and Big Mama looked at me then said to my grandfather, "you and Gina need to have a talk about that."

Pops headed up the stairs to find Laniyah and Gina.

I quietly asked my grandmother if she knew what Chris

"Trice, I'm in the sorority, you grandfather is in the fraternity, and quiet as it's kept, Christopher is also in the fraternity and he's the only that set Gina up in the first place for that damn orgy she did."

"How long has Pops known about it?"

"Long enough and he's handling it, but he wants Gina to talk to us about it."

"Got it. I just told her that she needed to talk to you about it and she said she would, I guess that time came quicker than she expected."

"I guess it did. Y'all staying here for the weekend?"

"Of course we are, we have to be back on campus for classes on Monday."

"Good, the five of us need to have a family discussion about Christopher and start healing, I never liked that boy."

"Are there any other siblings I need to know about?"

"Not that I know of; the plan when Chris's parents began raising Laniyah was that they would allow Chele and Brian to bring you to visit so the two of you could have a relationship, but them two ain't shit, which is why your grandfather and I don't bother with them cause their spirits ain't right. I'm just glad y'all have finally met and are forming a relationship."

"So am I Big Mama."

"So ladies, when is the probate?" Pops asked.

"I think it's two weeks from tomorrow if I'm not mistaken," Laniyah said looking through her phone.

"Great, we're going to make sure we come to support," Big Mama said.

"I'm going to let Aunt Chele and Uncle Brian know so they can decide whether or not they want to come up."

"Ma, you coming too, right?"
"I think it's best I sit this one out, I don't want to chance embarrassing y'all while I'm there."

"Gina, we'll be there, ain't no one dumb enough to try or say some shit out the side of their mouth while we're there, you're going," Pops said.

"Well, there you have it," Laniyah said, "we'll see y'all in two weeks, now what's for dinner?"

# The Freak in Me

For the next three hours the five of us sat at the dining table, talked, laughed, shed a few tears and played catch up with one another, the only person missing was JayVon, he was heavy on my mind so I sent him a text.

*"Hey handsome, hope all is well with you, you were on my mind. Hope to hear from you soon. Xoxoxo~Trice."*

After dinner I showered and went to bed, I was emotionally, physically, and mentally drained from the days events. For the next two days, Laniyah and I got to know one another better, found out we wee more alike than we realized. Gina spent some time with the both of us, together as well as individually and it was pretty dope getting to know and understand her.

As I was packing the car so we could head back to campus, Big Mama and Pops pulled me aside.

# Saige the Gemini

"Babygirl, your grandmother told me about the business idea you have for after you graduate."

"Do you think I'm in over my head with it? I feel like if we execute it right, we can turn a major profit and really become millionaires before we turn thirty."

"I think it's a brilliant idea, which is why your grandmother and I want to be the first to invest in it," he said while handing me a white envelope.

"Thank you so much! I don't even know how I'll ever repay you for this!"

"You ain't even look at the check!"
I slightly opened the envelope and I swore I was seeing things; I blinked my eyes a few times to bring them back in focus.

"Pops, I think you put too many numbers on this check."

"No I didn't, your eyes are seeing just fine."

# The Freak in Me

"Pops, this check is for five hundred thousand dollars."

"I know Trice, I wrote it."
I began to cry, like the ugly cry; never in my wildest dreams did I ever think this brainchild of mine would have a jumpstart like the one my grandparents just provided me. I gathered myself together, placed the envelope in my back pocket, hugged my grandparents and told them I'd see them in two weeks at my probate.

Gina pulled me to the side, "Trice, I just wanted to apologize again for all of the pain I've put you through over the years, I hope this weekend was the beginning of our healing journey and we will continue to keep in contact and continue healing."

"You're stuck with me honey! Ain't no way you're getting rid of me that easily, we're certainly going to keep in contact and I better see you in two weeks at my probate."

# Saige the Gemini

"I promise you'll see me there," she said smiling.

Laniyah said her see you laters to our grandparents and to our mother, we got in the car and headed back to Connecticut.

"So, what are your thoughts on this weekend?" Laniyah asked.

"For the most part, I think it went well, I think Christopher is a bitch made boy and he needs his ass whooped royally. What are your thoughts?"

"I wholeheartedly agree with you about Chris needing his ass handed to him, it felt good to be amongst family that genuinely care and loves you, this weekend was need for me, thank you for bringing me here."

"No thanks needed, you're family and if you don't have family, you don't have much of anything."

"True indeed."

# The Freak in Me

We rode the rest of the way singing at the top of our lungs, vibing out to my 90s R&B playlist.

## Two Weeks Later...

"Okay ladies, tonight is the night you've been waiting for, I know there were initially six of you, and only five are present tonight, but don't let the fact that one of your sisters isn't in attendance tonight stop you from having your moment. Are you ladies ready to be presented to the campus?" Soror SIYF asked.

We all said in unison, "Hell yea!!"
"All right ladies, masks on, heads up and let's get this show on the road!!" Soror ATM said.

"Greetings fellow ECU alum, students, staff and friends, tonight, we will introduce you to the newest members of Delta Pi Psi Sorority, Incorporated, are you ready?" Soror ATM greeted the crowd.

The crowd was going crazy, and Soror SIYF then said, "number one, introduce yourself!"

# Saige the Gemini

I stepped forward and said, "Good pussy is a blessing, but a woman with bomb pussy, crazy jaw and looks to kill is a triple threat, I'll all of that and then some, I am Soror Porn Star," I then took my mask off and revealed myself to my peers on campus.

I stepped back and Kiera stepped up then said, "Babyyyyy, I'm that chick that you can do anything with, you can smack me, flip me, and rub me down I'm all for it! My favorite position is when I'm on my hands and knees; I am Soror All Fours. When she took her mask off, everyone went crazy, some of the guys there had their mouths wide open, I guess 'cause Kiera is really a laid back type of chick.

When Kiera stepped up, Kyra stepped up, "Men love anal cause the ass is tight and it's different. Men love me because I love anal. My ass is tight like a virgins pussy; I am Soror Anal Princess. Kyra took her mask off and the guys started going crazy!

# The Freak in Me

Kyra stepped back and Marie stepped up, the crowd was waiting for her to speak but she just looked around, then out of nowhere she began laughing. She took her mask off first then said, "Ain't too much for me to say, everyone loves me, men and women. I'm the woman your girl loves to hate because her man can't get enough of me; I am Soror Kryptonite.

The guys were going crazy and some of the women were mean mugging the shit out of Marie, I mean, shorty was a sight to see.

Lastly, Jade stepped forward, she'd been a nervous wreck all day, I just hoped she'd be all right now that the spotlight was on her. All eyes were on her, and suddenly she began singing, "My melanin ain't nothing to fuck with! My pussy ain't nothing to fuck with! My ass ain't nothing to fuck with! My jaw ain't nothing to fuck with! My melanin, my melanin, my melanin, I am Soror Midnight Delight!"

# Saige the Gemini

I looked at my line sisters; they looked at me, then Soror ATM and Soror SIYF looked at all of us and we all began celebrating, then Soror ATM said, "Elm City University, here are the newest members of Delta Pi Psi Sorority, Incorporated! Ladies, you did the damn thing over this past month and change, so go celebrate and enjoy yourselves!"

My girls and I decided to go out and celebrate, but before we left, I went to check on Akira. It didn't feel right being initiated into Delta Pi Psi without my ace with me, but I totally understood why she couldn't be up there with us tonight.

I found my family and JayVon after probate was done, the looks on their faces were priceless.

"Congratulations Babygirl, you did the damn thing!" Jay said to me handing me two-dozen magenta, yellow and silver roses.

# The Freak in Me

"Thank you! I'm glad you were able to make it tonight," I told him before kissing him.

"If this probate didn't bring back some memories, I'd be lying," my aunt told me.

"I'm really glad all of you were able to make it on such short notice, it means the world to me," I told my family.

"You know we weren't going to miss this, this is major, where's your sister?" Gina said.

"She's around here somewhere, let me text her."

"They've changed this campus a hell of a lot since the last time we were here," Pops said looking around.

"Damn sure have, let's go look around," Big Mama said to Pops.

Right before they wandered off, Laniyah joined us. "Sis, you were phenomenal tonight!" she said hugging me.

"Thank you!!"

# Saige the Gemini

"What are y'all getting into tonight?" Aunt Chele asked.

"The girls and I are going out to celebrate, I gotta go check on my other sis first before though."

"Her other half is here," JayVon told me.

I looked at him with a concerned look.

"Relax, he knows nothing, I told him I was going to look around, I didn't want to be in the middle of whatever they had going on."

"Great, I hope to see you later tonight."

"You most definitely will," he said before kissing me.

Just as we broke our kiss, Xavier walked up to us.

"So, is this fool the reason you don't want to get back together?"

My family looked at Xavier like he was crazy, my Uncle Brian looked like he was ready to beat the brakes off of him.

"No, your dumbass is the reason I don't want to get back together, where's your girl Donise?"

"I don't know and she's not who I'm worried about right here, this guy right here is not good for you Trice."

"Listen here Xavier, I'm not the one you have an issue with, we don't even know one another like that, so watch your tone with her or you're going to have bigger problems."

"Wait, y'all know each other?"
"Yea, kinda, he was trying to get into BDM but I guess his dick wasn't big enough because right after the informational, he bounced."

I laughed, Jay ain't have to go in like that on Xavier but I'm glad he did, it felt good to have someone else tell Xavier off for me.

"Yo, whatever, we need to talk," Xavier said grabbing my arm.

Right then is when Uncle Brian stepped in.

# Saige the Gemini

"I don't know who you are you little punk but I think it's in your best interest to get the fuck off my niece and go on about your business, she's told you already she doesn't want to be bothered; now leave or you'll have bigger problems."

Xavier looked at Uncle Brian, then at JayVon then at me then said, "this ain't over Trice, your people ain't gonna be on campus all the time to protect you."

"Xavier, I promise you, my family is the least of your concern," I told him before my family and I left him standing in the quad like an idiot.

"You gonna be alright tonight Babygirl?" Uncle Brian asked.

"Yea, I'll be fine, Xavier is all talk, and remember, you raised me so I know how to put in work if I need to."

"That's my girl!"

# The Freak in Me

"Trice, we're in town for the next few days, so we can all link up for breakfast before we leave to go back home."

"Alright auntie, we can link tomorrow, I'm free all day, are you free tomorrow Laniyah?"

"Yes I am, I cleared my schedule for this week."

"Great, well you girls go have fun tonight, and we'll set up a time in the morning to get together," Aunt Chele said.

"See y'all in the morning!"

I stopped by my room to video chat Akira before we headed out to celebrate the night.

"So, Akira, what are you going to do now?"

"I'm going to have the baby, finish school and figure this parenting thing out as I go."

"The girls keep wondering why you dropped line all of a sudden, when are you going to tell them you're pregnant?"

# Saige the Gemini

"I'm not sure, I still haven't told Justice yet, shit, I haven't even told my parents yet, other than you, no one else knows."

"Wait, isn't Justice there?"

"He was, but we haven't been on the same page for a while and I'm not certain he's going to want me to keep the baby."

"Damn, well you know I'm here if you need anything."

I appreciate you Trice and that's on everything."

"You know you're stuck with me, ain't getting rid of me. What are you going to do about Delta Pi Psi?"

"I spoke with Big Sis ATM and Big Sis SIYF, they said something about doing private meet-ups, so I'm going to see how that goes."

"Keep me posted."

"You know I will, now you go enjoy your crossing party, I know the other ladies are probably

ing on you, oh wait, real quick, how did
probate go tonight?"

"It was crazy, yo, did you know Jade can
sing her ass off?"

"Hell no, she can?"
"Yea, she stunned us all when she introduced
herself."

"That's what's up! Text me when you get
back in so I'll know you made it back safely.

"Will do sis, love ya!"
"Love ya too!"

The rest of the girls and I decided to go to
Hollywood Cabaret Club to celebrate, I mean,
what better place than a strip club?

I went to this club by the name of The DyNasty Pleasure Palace; I was in dire need of something different tonight, Xavier and I just broke up, again and I needed to release this sexual tension.

I walked into the club wearing this black lace nightgown and a pair of black stilettos, I had one thing and one thing only on my brain, sex, sex with a chocolate god and his beautiful queen, that's right, you guessed it, The DyNasty Pleasure Palace is a swingers club, and I was going to get my rocks off hard tonight!

I mixed my own drink as the club was BYOB, made me a simple rum and coke, I sat at the bar and allowed the music and the alcohol to take me into another world mentally. After my third drink, I went and sat next to this beautiful couple who kept eyeing me from the time I walked into the club, the husbands body looked

# The Freak in Me

as if he were God himself and the wife, my gawd, her body was the color of honey, only bad thing was, I couldn't see their faces as they had masks on.

If their faces matched their bodies, I was good with that. Shortly after I joined them on the couch, the mystery man wasted no time in removing his penis from his pants; just the sight of it made me wet and my mouth salivate more than usual. As I started topping him off his woman came around and started eating me like I was soul food on Thanksgiving night. I moaned in pure ecstasy from a combination of sucking his dick and being eaten out. I was starting to wonder why I wasted so much time with Xavier; this is something we argued about on so many occasions.

After a good twenty minutes of sucking dick, he slid on a Durex XXL condom and entered me, I think I had died and gone to Heaven, his stroke was just the right tempo, and the fact that I was able to eat his woman's sweet box was an added bonus. She not only had the skin tone of honey, but she tasted like it too, I wonder if they'd consider letting me be their girlfriend. I orgasmed five times just from being fucked and if I counted correctly, the mystery woman came six times from me eating her out. The guy then took his condom off and had his woman mount him, and now it was my turn to feel how his tongue felt against my pussy.

Watching this woman ride her man's dick was an amazing sight to see, I knew my next move was to sex her, I had to, her body was too fine for me not to fuck her.

Watching them make love to one another the way they did almost had me missing Xavier, this is what I wanted to experience with him, but he would never budge. Anyway, just as this god in human form was about to cum his woman and I both got on our knees so we could both taste it; after he came, her and I embraced in a long, sensual kiss, and her hands started traveling up my body and mine on hers. The kiss was like no other I had ever experienced; it was as if we were the only two people in the room, no one else at that moment mattered but her and I. We laid on the couch, me on top and her beneath me, we began to feast on one another, when she tapped me on my ass, I knew she wanted to feel my love box against hers, so I obliged her. Y'all know she wasn't the first woman I've slept with but she's the first I kind of felt a connection with.

We scissored one another, then I spread her legs and fucked her from the front, her facial expressions were priceless, I knew she was enjoying me as much as I was enjoying her, I was hoping for this night never ended. We both climaxed together, I fell on top of her; her man came too, we noticed he was cleaning himself off after we finished.

I went to the bathroom to freshen up, got dressed and on my way out, the mystery man

# Saige the Gemini

said to me, "We hope to see you next week sexy." My only response was a wink of the eye. I wasn't yet certain I wanted this to be an ongoing thing with these two.

Once I got in my car, I sent Xavier a text message asking if we could talk, I missed my love....

Xavier texted me back ASAP and he told me to meet him at his house, he was out with his guys drinking and was on his way back home. When I got to his house, I was nervous all of a sudden and I didn't know why; just thinking about him gave me butterflies.

He pulled into his driveway about five minutes after I arrived and when he stepped out in a crisp white tee, dark wash denim jeans and crisp white Nike's, I instantly got wet. "No fuckin' tonight, Trice, you are just here to talk, nothing more," I told myself.

Xavier came to my car door and opened it for me and helped me out of the car.

# The Freak in Me

"Damn Trice, where you coming from? You look damn good tonight."

"I went to The DyNasty Pleasure Palace, nothing too special."

"The DyNasty? Isn't that a swingers club?"

"Sure is..." I kept my answer short and sweet; I knew he'd be upset just thinking about me fucking someone else.

"Let's go in the house so we can talk," he told me as he grabbed my waist and we walked to his front door together.

When we got into the house, I walked up the stairs and made myself comfortable on his bed, shoes off and everything, I already knew I wasn't going home tonight.

He went to his bar, made us both a drink and came into his room handed me my drink and asked, "So, what did you want to talk about?"

## Saige the Gemini

"Us, I legit miss you, and I hate admitting this shit," I told him while I downed the rum and Coke he made me.

"You broke up with me Trice, you needed your space and wasn't ready for all that I was, do you not remember that? We want some of the same things in life and I wanted to provide you with that, but you weren't ready."

"I know and for that I'm honestly sorry, I want you and only you, I love you, no one makes my heart skip a beat like you do, no one gives me butterflies like you do, I crave you like none other, you are on my mind nonstop, and I never want to not have you on my mind."

He stood silent for about five minutes then left his room. I sat up on the bed looking and feeling like I poured my heart out to one of the only men I loved only for him to leave me.

After a good three minutes or so he returned to the room and just stared at me, then embraced my face in his, then told me, "come shower with me."

I obliged, I needed to wash my sexcapades from the DyNasty Pleasure Palace off of me before Xavier and I did whatever was on his mind tonight.  Xavier started the water in the shower, lit candles all around the bathroom; I guess he was missing me as much as I was missing him. He helped me undress, took his time in looking at every inch of my body. He then helped me into the shower then got undressed and joined me, he washed my back, I was his, and then he entered me from the back.

"Where's your condom?"
"Trice, do we really need a condom? I need to feel all of you while I'm inside."

"Are you really trying to chance getting me pregnant tonight?"

"Baby, we've talked about getting married and having children, we can practice now." I said nothing more; I just enjoyed this time with him.

# Saige the Gemini

He slow stroked my pussy as if he were savoring every moment, his hands moved from my waist, he cupped each of my breasts, I reached back and grabbed the back of his head with one hand and started massaging his dick with the other. My legs began shaking uncontrollably and he released his load into me shortly after. We showered, again and made our way back to the bedroom. Before I could dry off, Xavier sat me on the bed, gently laid me back and began kissing me; he was still hard as a rock. His kisses began on my lips then traveled south, making sure he left no part of my body untouched. He entered me, as I was cumming again, he loved torturing me with sex, and I can't front, I loved it too.

# The Freak in Me

## The next morning

I woke Xavier up to breakfast and head, this was something I could get used to, waking up to the man I loved and that loved me. I sucked the first nut outta him then we had a quickie before we started our day. "Trice, tell me about The DyNasty last night, what was it like?"

"It's a real chill spot, very nice ambiance, the couples there last night were cool.

"You don't have to answer this next question if you don't want to, but did you fuck anyone last night?"

"Honestly? I did, it was a couple that I felt a connection with as soon as I walked in. When we linked eyes, I knew it was on from that moment on with them."

"Did you enjoy yourself? Did you fuck both of them?"

# Saige the Gemini

"I did, but when the guy and I fucked, he wrapped it up, you know I don't play that."

"Ok."

"What's that look for? You sound upset."

"I guess I'm just wondering if that is something that you're going to want to do on a regular."

"If we are getting back together then I wouldn't disrespect you and go by myself or fuck anyone else."

"I appreciate your honesty. I would like to experience it with you at least once, just to see how it is and how I feel."

"I would love that, and if you're not comfortable with it, we don't ever have revisit it."

"What did I do to deserve you?"

"I don't know but if you keep making me as happy as you have been, you're going to have a hard time getting rid of me."

"That's never going to happen."

# The Freak in Me

Xavier and I made love one more time then we
our separate ways.

Xavier sent me a text message asking me if I wanted to go to The DyNasty with him. I asked if he was sure he wanted to go, he said yea, so I got dressed in this red sheer fishnet garter set, and my nipples were so perky, they snuck straight through the fishnets. Xavier wore a black wife beater and a pair of black silk pajama bottoms; we were ready to have fun tonight. I can't and won't lie tho, the thought of watching him fuck another woman made me so uneasy, I was beginning to have second thoughts about going through with tonight, he must've seen the apprehension on my face.

"Bae, you alright? Looks like something is bothering you."

"Honestly, the thought of you fuckin another woman in front of me is kind of making me sick to my stomach."

"We don't have to go if you don't feel comfortable with it, I can see it's making you visibly upset."

"You can still go if you want, I'll go back home."

"Absolutely not, we either go together or not at all, we can stay in and do whatever you want to do."

What did he tell me that for?

All the while we were showering and getting dressed all my mind was thinking about was taking his dick in my mouth, gaggin on it, riding it and having it in my ass.

"How about we make a movie tonight?"

His eyebrows went up, as if to say, "Word?"

"Walk with me to my car, I have my camera equipment in there, we gonna be on some professional shit tonight."

## Saige the Gemini

His dick sprang straight up, it was clear to me then that he had on no drawers. We set the camera up and before I could get my underwear off or even start the camera, he ripped them and stuffed all six and three quarter inches of his dick in me. It took all of five minutes for Xavier to bust his first nut, he released his load right inside of me; and part of me was ok with it and part of me knew the chances of that nut being the one to get me pregnant was pretty high.

"X, you know when you don't wear a condom, you're supposed to pull out."

"Would us getting pregnant right now be so bad?"

"Hell yea it would be, we're in an awkward space right now."

"I'm not sure why, we love one another, you know I don't want to spend my life with anyone else but you, do you not feel the same way?"

# The Freak in Me

"I do, I think, but I still think it's too early for us to start a family."

Instead of responding, Xavier kissed me deeply, lifted me onto his shoulders and ate my box like he was famished.

## Two days later...

I had a feeling that X really got me pregnant, but until it was time for me to find out, I really wanted to experience The DyNasty with him, so I sent him a text message.

*"Babe let's try DyNasty tonight, I want to see you out of your comfort zone, and I promise I won't back out like I did the other night, LOL, hit me back when you get this."*

## 10 minutes later....

*"Hey love, I was just about to text you, you've been on my mind. If you're comfortable*

with it, I say let's do it, like I said before if it's something we're not too fond of, we never have to go back, if it's something we like, we can go occasionally. What time would you like for me to pick you up?"

"I should be ready by 9:30, make sure you wear something sexy for me daddy."

"Keep it up and it'll be a repeat of the other night, we ain't be going anywhere."

"Oh no, we're definitely going out tonight, something about watching you fuck another woman is making me wet just thinking about it."

"Trice, you know I'm at work, I'm about to have to take an extended lunch and come break you off really quick, you got me hard as fuck right now."

"I'm rubbing my wet pussy just thinking about it baby. Damn she's wet."

"Keep her wet for daddy, he's about to come over and tend to her needs really quick."

# The Freak in Me

*"Aht, aht, save all that for tonight; on my way home I'll pick up extra condoms, just in case."*

*"You do that shit purposely, get me rock hard then bail on me. That ass is mine tonight, and I mean that literally."*

*"Lol, I don't know what you're talking about. Love you boo, talk to you later on."*

## Later that night...

"Trice, you ready?"

"Yes, just finished putting my shoes on.

Xavier came into the room and grabbed me by my waist.

"Damn baby, you look good as fuck."

"You don't look too bad yourself baby."

"You still sure you want to go tonight?"

# Saige the Gemini

"Yes, I've thought long and hard about it and visions of you deep stroking another chick is making me wet as shit right now."

"Only one rule for tonight for you, no swallowing another guy, I gotta draw the limit somewhere with you, and you cannot put your mouth on another guy."

"Fair enough, but same goes for you, no eating any bitches out tonight."

"You never have to worry about that. Let's go shorty, time to have some fun."

When Xavier and I got to DyNasty the couple I had my encounter with the last time I was here and I made instant eye contact, I whispered to X that they were the couple that I was with when I came the last time. They motioned for us to join them, we made our formal introductions, poured a few drinks and once the drinks started flowing in our system, it was on!

Out of nowhere the woman kissed me, caught me off guard a little but I didn't push her away, our kiss intensified, she started cupping my breasts with one hand and the other was fingering my already wet box.

Out of the corner of my eye I saw Xavier getting quite excited, his dick was standing up as far as his pajama pants allowed. X took his member out of his pants and playfully slapped me on my face with it before putting it in my mouth. The god in human form kneeled in front of his woman and began dining on her. She slowly removed her hand from my love box and licked her fingers until all of my juices were gone; she then kissed me so we could share the taste.

The Adonis put a condom on and pulled me over to him, when he entered me, I could do nothing but gasp, his length and width was unmatched. His woman got on all fours, X put his condom on and slowly entered her, her face said it all, she was about to enjoy Xavier almost as much as I do on a daily. As Xavier was diggin' her out from the back and the guy had me

# Saige the Gemini

missionary, Marie and I embraced in a kiss, then she proceeded to lick my clit, her licks and his strokes were so in sync, it was driving me wild. I had no choice but to return the favor, it was pure ecstasy. The four of us climaxed together, it was such an experience.

# The Freak in Me

## Two Days Later...

"Babe, are you up for another night at DyNasty?"

"Sure, I'm surprised you liked it as much as you did."

"I didn't think I would but something about seeing another dude pleasuring you turned me on."

"You sure you won't regret it later on?"

"I don't think I will. Question for you."

"Answer for you."

"What do you think about inviting that couple over, we can be more intimate with them without the stipulations and rules of the club?"

"So, you basically want to do like a partner swap with them on the regular?"

"Possibly, is that something you'd consider?"

# Saige the Gemini

"Hell no!"

"Why do you sound like you're upset now?"

"You're basically telling me I'm not enough for you and you want a pass to fuck another bitch whenever you feel like it."

"Do you not like how that guy fucks you?"

"I do, but with him it's just sex, it's not like what I thought we had, passion, love. When we're intimate, that's just what we have, intimacy. What we do with that couple is just fuckin' no feelings attached, or at least I thought that's what it was."

"Got it," Xavier replied pissed as fuck; he just knew I would be down with inviting that couple to our bedroom every once in a while.

I got up from the kitchen table, took a quick shower, got dressed and left Xavier's house without speaking another word to him. X bruised my ego just a lil, he made me feel as if I wasn't enough for him, and I now regretted exposing X to the DyNasty.

# The Freak in Me

I drove to my house in complete silence, I needed to talk and there were only two people I trusted, and one of them was dealing with their own problems so I called the other.

"What's up love?" The person on the other end answered.

"Hey, you, are you busy right now?"

"Nope, just left my brothers crib, what's up?"

"I need to bend your ear for a little while."

"You want to come to my place, or do you want me to come to yours?"

"You can come to my place, if you don't mind."

"I'll be there in five minutes."
"The door will be unlocked, just come on in."

"Bet."
When Jay got to my house he walked right in and saw me sitting at the bar with a drink in my hand.

# Saige the Gemini

"Uh oh, you drinking this early in the day means one of two things, either someone just died or you and ya man got into an argument."

"It's definitely the latter," I said turning my seat so I could face Jay.

"Tell daddy all about it," he responded.

I smirked and replied, "You're so damn stupid. Anyway, long story short, last week X and I went to the club, big mistake cause now he wants to invite Marie and Julius into our personal space and do some partner swap type shit with them."

"You knew there was a chance of that happening though, right?"

"Hell no! I thought we were solid, like, we'd go, do our thing and that would be it."

"Does X know you and Marie are line sisters? Does he know y'all own the club?"

# The Freak in Me

"Nah, only people that know are the ones that need to know."

"So, what are you going to do?"

"Honestly? I'm ready to walk away from him, like, if one night out fuckin' other people makes him instantly want to bring them into our lives on a regular basis, that tells me I'm not enough for him and I'm not about to waste more time in my life with someone who needs more than one woman pleasing him."

Jay looked at me and I could tell by his facial expression that he felt bad for me cause me and Xavier had been together almost as long as Akira and Justice have been together. Jay always knew he was the better choice for me, but he didn't want to seem like he was hating on my relationship, so he just let me rock.

"What do you think I should do? You and Akira are the two that know me the best and I value your opinion."

# Saige the Gemini

"You know I always keep it a buck with you when you ask for my input. I'll tell you this; you know X has stepped out on you before, regardless of how long ago it was. Most of the time X is the type of guy to go get what he wants, no matter if it hurts others or not. The both of you have a long ass history together, so I'll put it like this, if the good outweighs the bad, I say stick with him, but if you feel as if you're not going to be able to trust him, dead it right now."

"I'm going to see if he ends up at the club without me tonight, if he does and fucks someone else, I'm done."

"Fair enough, do you really think he's going to go without you?"

"Hell yea. Matter of fact, I'm going to go myself but be in the owners suite, you know I can see everything that goes on in the club from up there unbeknownst to everyone else, and if he pulls up, I'm going to end it in the morning."

# The Freak in Me

"You a sneaky mothafucka and I love every minute of it," Jay said laughing.     "Hit me tomorrow after everything and let me know what happened."

"You know I will."

"Cool. Yo, how you and Akira business owners?"

"She's one of my line sisters in DPP."

"Get the fuck outta here!! Are you bullshittin' me right now?"

"Not at all, Marie, Kiera, Jade, Kyra and I all crossed at the same time. You didn't know?!"

"Fuck no! I wonder if my brother knows."

"Don't say shit to him about it, that's for her to tell him, not anyone else. If she found out I told anyone, including you, she'd probably stop talking to me."

"I got you love; my lips are sealed."

"Let me go get myself together, boss mode tonight. You behave yourself tonight please."

"We are always on our best behavior."

# Saige the Gemini

"Negro, I know you, so I know that's a lie," I said laughing.

"Hit me tomorrow, got something I want to talk to you about."

"Alright love, let's do lunch or something tomorrow."

"You got it, my treat," Jay responded as he was finishing his drink before standing up to give me a hug.

I walked Jay to the door, went back to my bar to finish my drink then proceeded to my room to get ready for tonight, I felt it in my gut that Xavier was going to be on some bullshit tonight.

I sent Marie a text message and told her if Xavier came in tonight play like everything's cool, I wanted to see if he was going to go straight to them or another couple. Marie hit me back immediately and told me she had my back.

# The Freak in Me

## Six hours later...

I entered the club using the underground entrance. I gathered my belongings from the trunk, locked the car, and then took the elevator to the owner's suite of the club.

The club began filling up with a lot of the regulars, and an influx of single men and women. I loved the fact that my line sisters and I had the idea in college to start a swingers club together. The club was making a killing and the Seductive Six were on their way to becoming millionaires before we turned thirty.

Tonight was the clubs annual *What's Your Fantasy* night, anything and everything was allowed. This was a night where women who have fantasized about being with another woman had their fantasy come true. This was one of the clubs highest paid nights, I smiled while looking at all of the patrons, and tonight was going to be epic in more ways than one.

I checked my phone to see if Xavier bothered to call or text me, no missed notifications.

"He's going to be on some bullshit tonight, I already know it," I said aloud. I popped open a bottle of Baileys Strawberries and Cream, poured a little in a glass and sat at my desk.

Just as I powered on my laptop, my main bodyguard Lance sent a text to me that read, "*he's here*." I responded, "*showtime*."

I kept my eyes on Xavier and every move he made and the many times he violated.

"Hey handsome, my name is Kiera, I see you're here all alone, care for some company?"

"Absolutely beautiful, my name is Xavier, it's nice to meet you."

"The pleasure is all mine. The club is packed tonight, do you come here often?"

# The Freak in Me

"Nah, this is my second time here. My girl and I came together not to ago, and now I want to experience it by myself."

"She's not going to be upset with you for coming here without her?"

"What she doesn't know can't hurt her."

"So, what's your fantasy tonight?" "You," Xavier responded taking his already hard dick out of his pants.

Kiera's eyes widened at the site of his dick. She reached to the small bowl of condoms that was situated right next to where she was seated.

"No condom necessary, unless you want to use it," he told Kiera.

"I would rather feel and experience all of you, I just wanted to be respectful."

"You're good luv, I'm clean, you won't catch anything from me."

Kiera got up and walked in front of X, took her nightgown off and exposed her beautiful chocolate C cup breasts. She knelt down in front of Xavier and first put just the head of his dick in her mouth, then she went in for the kill and devoured him.

Xavier was enjoying every moment of his dick in Kiera's mouth. As she was sucking him off, she began fingering herself and X was playing with and caressing her titties.

"Damn baby, suck that dick, you like this shit, don't you?"

"Hell yea daddy, your dick is so big, big dicks make me extra wet," she responded as she slid her fingers out of her drippin' wet pussy and put them in Xavier's mouth. Xavier took his time savoring Kiera's taste, then kissed her deeply.

After another ten minutes of getting his dick sucked, Xavier stood Kiera up and placed her on the couch with her butt hanging off just a little. He kneeled in front of her and licked her pussy slowly, then he slowly stuck his tongue inside of her while placing one of his fingers inside her asshole.

# The Freak in Me

Kiera's legs began shaking uncontrollably, she loved anal play and to be getting eaten out and having her ass played with at the same time, she was in heaven.

As Kiera and Xavier were enjoying one another, I was watching their interaction and from the moment Xavier allowed Kiera to stick his dick in her mouth, I knew Xavier was out for self and our time together was over.

*"Meet me at my house in ten minutes,"* I sent a text to Jay.

I gathered my belongings, hopped on the elevator, and left the club, I'd seen all I needed to see.

Just as I was pulling into my garage, Jay was pulling up; I motioned for him to pull all the way into the garage.

"I thought we were linking for lunch tomorrow, what happened?"

"We're still doing lunch tomorrow but tonight, we're doing each other."

# Saige the Gemini

"Trice, talk to me love, what happened?"

"He was at the club tonight and violated in the worst way. He allowed Kiera to suck his dick, something we promised to one another we wouldn't let happen, I wasn't supposed to go down on another man and another woman wasn't supposed to go down on him, he didn't even have the common courtesy to put a condom on before Kiera sucked him off."

"Wait, Kiera as in your line sister?"

"The one and only."

"Damn, I'm sorry love," Jay said looking concerned.

"Eight years down the drain cause of his bullshit; I'm just happy I saw his true colors for myself," I said as I headed to my bar to pour myself a drink.

Jay joined me at the bar and poured himself a glass of White Hennessy.

"What are you going to do now?"

"You," I said as I began undressing.

# The Freak in Me

"Trice, I don't want to be your rebound guy."

"You're not Jay, I've wanted you to myself since the first time we met. Our friendship has blossomed over the years and quite honestly, our sexual chemistry is just fuckin' remarkable. You get me and other than my business partners, you're my best friend, and I'm in love with you." Jay knew I wouldn't toy with his feelings and I hope he felt in his heart that I was telling him the truth.

Jay threw his drink back in one swallow, by this time; I was sitting on top of the bar in only my bra and panties. The mere sight of me sitting there with no clothes on, my hair slightly covering my left eye had Jay in a trance.

He picked me up, carried me to my bedroom and gently laid me on my bed. He pulled a condom out of his back pocket, put it on and slowly entered my wet, throbbing pussy.

# Saige the Gemini

I moaned, "Pussy Monster," as he entered my sweet spot.

"Tonight I'm either Jay or baby, no Pussy Monster, do you understand?" Jay told me, as he was slow stroking me.

"Yes baby, keep going nice and slow just like that," I managed to say before the first orgasm ripped through my body, my legs shaking uncontrollably.

As Jay was slow stroking me, he began sensually kissing me, something we'd never really done during their fuck sessions. Once I was able to somewhat gain control back of my body, I began matching Jay's thrusts with thrusts of my own; we were in sync.

Forty-five minutes after we began, we climaxed together. Jay laid beside me and pulled me closer to him.

"Let me find out you like cuddling!"
"Truth be told, you're the only woman I've ever cuddled with, it's something about you that

allows me to be Jay and not have to live up to my frat name."

"You know you don't have to always be in Pussy Monster mode when you're around women."

"Try telling them that, it's like they expect me to be in Pussy Monster mode all the time, it's tiring."

Well listen, you know around me, you can be the JayVon Duarte I met years ago," I told him.

"I appreciate you baby girl, I really do."

Just as we were on our way to the bathroom my phone rings and I immediately rolled my eyes, I knew it was Xavier.

"You not going to answer it?"

"Hell no, I have nothing to say to him after what I saw tonight, I'm good on him, like Mya said, I'll be moving on."

"I respect it, do you shorty. You joining me in the shower before I go home?"

# Saige the Gemini

"You tryin' to get another session poppin' you're not slick," I responded as I dropped my robe.

"I just wanted you to help me wash my back, that's all, get ya mind outta the gutter."

"If you say so sir, now are we showering together or what?"

# The Freak in Me

## The next morning

As I was making my morning tea my doorbell rings, I looked at my camera system; it was the last person I wanted to see, Xavier. I rolled her eyes and reluctantly opened the door.

"Hey love, I've been calling and texting you since last night, how are you?"

"I'm better now, what's up with you?

"I think we should talk about the argument we had, we've never argued and gone more than a few hours without saying a word to one another."

"You're right, we should talk, let me start. Xavier, I'm done with you, I never want to see you again, you are a low life piece of shit and I'm happy I'm not carrying your baby. I regret the day I mentioned going to the DyNasty with you, that right there was my fault, but allowing the lust to overtake you, that's all on you."

## Saige the Gemini

Xavier interrupted and said, "Trice, what are you talking about? I love you baby! I want to do life with you, why are you saying all of this?"

"I saw you at the club last night, you disrespected me and our relationship, you let another woman go down on you and you fucked her raw! But you say you love me? What the fuck does love to have to do with it? If that's your version of love, I want no parts of it."

Xavier stood there looking defeated, he didn't know what to say or do. His intent wasn't to hurt me, he just needed some him time, but it backfired on him. He'd fucked up royally and he knew there was no coming back from it.

"The only thing I can say is I'm sorry Trice, and I know that's not enough. I did and still do cherish the time we were together, and I have no one to blame but myself for our relationship ending."

"Get the fuck out of my house, good riddance and I wish you a life you of everything you deserve you cheating piece of shit!" I yelled then told Siri to play *Irreplaceable* by Beyoncé.

Xavier hung his head low and walked out of my house and life. He knew he'd fucked up he just didn't think his secret would be exposed not even twenty-four hours later.

As I was on my way back to my bedroom, Jay was descending the stairs.

"You alright baby girl?"
"I'm great! Never felt better. You on your way home?"

"Yea, don't want to overstay my welcome."

"You're always welcomed here," I told him before kissing him.

"Don't start making me feel like you got a love jones for me."

"There's no secret that I've had feelings for you for a long time, the timing was never right, until now."

# Saige the Gemini

"I don't want to be your rebound guy Trice, that's not my style."

"You're not my rebound guy, I feel in my heart that you're my forever guy. You're my best male friend, you know me just about as well as I know myself, I don't expect us to be in a relationship tomorrow but maybe it's something we can work on?"

"We'll talk about it some more tomorrow night over dinner. I'm 'bout to eat breakfast then break out."

"What do you want me to make for break..."

Before I could finish my question, Jay picked me up, sat me on my couch, took my robe off and began planting small kisses all over my body. He started on my neck and traveled all the down to my feet, then traveled back up until he got to my sweet spot. As he was eating me out, he began stroking his dick, the sounds I was making was turning him on.

# The Freak in Me

After twenty minutes of eating me out Jay entered me gently, and I began shaking immediately.

"Jay, Jay, wait..."

Jay put his finger over my mouth to quiet me; he just wanted us to enjoy one another before he had to leave.

Fifteen minutes later we climaxed together.

"Jay, you can't keep fuckin' me like this."

"Sweetheart, when we're together we don't fuck, we make love, remember that. Now I gotta go, don't forget, we're going to dinner tomorrow."

"Yes, Pussy Monster," I replied playfully.

## Saige the Gemini
## Six Months Later

JayVon and I have been going strong, I've always felt in my heart that he was the man for me but when you're young and a little ignorant you make ignorant decisions. The love between the both of us is something amazing, and let me let y'all in on a little secret, we're expecting twins, but I haven't told him yet, so let's keep this to ourselves…until we meet again!

Oh and this isn't the last you're going to hear about the DyNasty Pleasure Palace either, we've got some freaky and sexy shit cumming, oops, I mean coming your way soon, so be on the look out.

*Smooches…xoxoxo Trice, a.k.a. Soror Porn Star*

# The Freak in Me

Saige the Gemini

# The Freak in Me

## Coming soon from the Authors at

Bruised Never Broken: Letters to my Ex's is the final installment of Rocky Rose's *My Man My Abuser* series. Qortni Monroe pens letters to all of her ex men, ex abusers, ex situationships and ex fuck buddies.

Qortni is currently on her healing journey and she's no longer in the same headspace as she was when she penned *Stirred and Shaken*, so her approach to the finale is a little different than the first to books in the series.

Come take the final ride with Qortni and see what she's penned to her ex's as well as a few other's from her past that were introduced to you in *My Man My Abuser*.

# The Freak in Me

Pastor and First Lady Blake are on their way to retiring and their very promiscuous son Ronald is next in line to be head pastor at Agape Love Christian Church. Before Ronald can take the role of pastor, he has to be married. Ronald and his cousin go out one night to Ace or Diamonds Gentlemen's Club and there is where Ronald meets his future wife, Tyra Mitchell. Tyra is a stripper with a colorful past and her past doesn't faze Ronald but ruffles many at the church. Ronald, Tyra and the Blake family must go through hell and back to gain the trust of the members of the church and get them to accept Tyra as their new First Lady.

# Saige the Gemini

You were introduced to Akira in Initiation, as Justice's wife, but there's a lot you don't know about her background and her initiation into Delta Pi Psi Sorority. Akira is the child of a pastor and minister and the only child, growing up, her father was strict on her, which didn't allow her to do much hanging out when she was younger. When Akira got to college, it was a girls gone wild experience for her, and by chance, she ended up pledging Delta Pi Psi Sorority, and hides it from her parents and her then boyfriend, Justice. Are you ready for Soror Throat Doctor?

# The Freak in Me

Females playing football used to be unheard of, but for 17-year-old Phoenix Bacote, football has been a love of hers since she learned how to walk. When Phoenix showed up to her high school's teams practice, football MVP, Jaxon Antrum, was floored when he saw how great Phoenix was on the turf. Getting to know one another on and off the field, both Phoenix and Jaxon begin to fall in love with one another. Right before their high school graduation, they find out they've been accepted to different colleges on football scholarships, and they question if their brand-new relationship can handle being so far apart.

# Saige the Gemini
## In Case You Missed These:

***I Win You Lose*** is a compilation of six short stories all dealing with different aspects of domestic violence.

# The Freak in Me

My Man My Abuser introduces you to a vibrant nineteen-year-old Qortni Monroe who is holding down two jobs, has dreams and aspirations for her future. In the summer of 2004 Qortni meets Qamar Daniels, a twenty-year-old who really has nothing going for himself, not even in the looks department.

Qamar has low self-esteem, has no real goals for his life; he's just winging it. When he meets Qortni, he kinda falls head over heels for her, but unfortunately the feelings are mutual right away.

In their three-year relationship there are many fights, arguments, heartbreak and broken promises, will these two weather the storm or will their relationship crumble and fall?

Qortni Monroe is back, question is, has she learned her lesson or has she found herself in a similar predicament? Qortni and Qamar is no doubt an absolute wrap and being the smooth operator he is, Tony Wilson steps right up to the plate to help Qortni really get over Qamar.

Tony was introduced to you in My Man My Abuser and him and Qortni formed a special friendship. He was the shoulder to lean on, the chest to cry on and the listening ear Qortni needed during her relationship with Qamar. Qortni falls head over heels in love with Tony, question is, is he an older, more seasoned version of Qamar?

**God Made Me Special**

Written by : Ajia Lewis & Rocky Rose

Based on a true story, God Made Me Special takes you through the journey of a determined little girl who undergoes surgery so she can finally walk.

# Saige the Gemini

Initiation takes you on the journey of Jay-Von and Justice Duarte who are both members of Beta Delta Mu Fraternity Inc. They find out there is an elite division of their fraternity and they have been invited to join, but with stipulations. Justice is the married twin of the brothers and his wife, Akira, a pastor's daughter, have a pretty good marriage, except for the fact that she never goes down on Justice. Akira has a few skeletons of her own, ones that neither her parents nor her husband know anything about. During Justice and JayVon's initiation weekend, secrets will be exposed and tough decisions will be made. Will Akira and Justice's marriage survive? Will Akira's secrets be exposed?

# The Freak in Me

## In case you missed it….The book that started it all!!

## Initiation

"Justice baby, keep hittin' that spot there baby! Oh, My Gawd!! You're about to make me cum!!"

"Baby, your pussy is so damn wet! Where can I bust this nut?"

"Don't pull out, please, let's cum together," Akira said before another orgasm ripped through her body.

"Ahhhhhhhhh!!!" Akira and I screamed at the same time as we climaxed together.

"Kira, there's no way ya pops will let you go to school in Georgia?"

## Saige the Gemini

"Nope, I've begged, pleaded, and even tried to reason with him, it's a no-go bae."

"Damnit, what does ya moms think about you going out of state?"

"She's all for it, she's even been talking to my father about it for me but he's just not budging. I kinda think he knows if I move to Georgia for school I'm not coming back here to live."

"Fuck! So, what are we going to do about us? You know staying in Connecticut after school for me was never the plan, but I don't want to leave you."

"Do you think we can make a long-distance relationship work? Or do you think we should just go our separate ways? I don't want you to feel obligated to me while you're in Georgia."

"Kira, I plan on marrying you once we graduate so breaking up is not an option for me. I think if we both want the relationship to work, we can do the long-distance thing."

"You really want to marry me?"

"I'd marry you tomorrow if I could love. I think we've decided then; we'll visit one another during our breaks and if your parents will allow it, I can spend Thanksgiving here with you and for Christmas break you can come to Georgia and spend it with Jay and I."

## Saige the Gemini

"I'm with it; I really think we can make it work; communication will be key in making it work bae."

"We'll be aight, maybe after a year or so ya pops will loosen his grip on you and you'll be able to transfer, either way, you're stuck with me," I told Kira while playfully hitting her on her ass.

# The Freak in Me
## Two months later in Atlanta

"Bruhhhhhhhh, Atlanta is more than I ever imagined! And do you see the women down here? Got damn!"

"Jay, the last thing on my mind is the women down here, did you forget I'm with Akira? She's my one and only, the only one I have my eyes on."

"You sound whipped J; I'll just have to have enough fun for the both of us while we're down here."

## Saige the Gemini

"As long as you keep up with your grades, I don't give a damn how much fun you have, just remember our end goal is to get that diploma."

"Yea, yea, you know when it comes to the edumacation, I got that on lock, so don't even worry. I do remember what mama and daddy had in their will regarding our inheritance, I'm only two minutes younger than you boy."

"Just know that our inheritance is dependent on both of us walking that stage and getting our diplomas. So, if one of us fucks up, we fuck it up for the both of us."

My brother and I sat in silence for what seemed like an eternity, we had never really spoken about the loss of our parents to anyone, not even amongst ourselves, it was rather

difficult to discuss, even with each other. Just a

quick backstory on our parents untimely

passing, it was the summer leading up to me

and Jay's senior year in high school, one of our

cousins on our father's had a going away party

for his son's departure to college. My parents

were lightweights when it came to drinking and

for some reason or another, they thought they'd

be able to hang with our cousins who drink any

day that ends in y and any time that ends with

o'clock or thirty. Either way, after my parents

were rather saucy, they thought it would be a

good idea to take the hour drive back home but

never made it; they merged onto the highway

going the wrong way and an eighteen-wheeler

collided with them before either driver had

time to break or try to avoid the accident. My

parents were killed instantly, and because of

their prior investments and good choices in

business, it left our brother and I with more

than enough money to pay for their funeral,

bury them, pay for their headstones, and still

live comfortably and a bonus, they left us both a

hefty inheritance that we can only receive once

we get our college degrees.

"You good J? You got quiet and started

staring off."

I wiped a tear from my eye and replied,

"yea, I'm good, just can't believe mama and pops

won't be here to see us get our degrees again, it didn't seem real at our high school graduation and it's not going to seem real when we walk for our college graduation either."

"It sucks big time bro, to the point where I almost don't want to drink anymore, just imaging the scene of the accident still gives me nightmares and remember when the state troopers came to the house to tell us the horrible news," JayVon said wiping tears from his eyes.

"One thing for sure and two for certain, we got through it all with each other, and we'll continue to have each other's backs as we get through life without our parents. They've instilled a lot of knowledge, positivity, and great

values in us, so we'll be good."

"True indeed, but enough of this sad talk,

let's see what this campus has to offer before

classes start later this week."

JayVon and I locked up our apartment and

decided to see what Atlanta University's

campus had to offer. When we got to the

campus, different Greek organizations had

booths for perspective pledges, some of the D9

orgs were out in full swing, the Ques were

strolling, the Deltas were strolling, it was

amazing, but there were a group of guys that

had on their organizations paraphernalia but

had no booth, they stood out to me the most, they caught my brother's eye too.

The organizations name was Beta Delta Mu, they donned black jackets with red and gold writing, one thing I do know for sure is that they aren't apart of the Divine 9, which is why I think they stood out to my brother and me.

"J, do you see what I'm seeing?"

"If you're talking bout the brothers of Beta Delta Mu, yea, I peeped them as soon as we came out here. You thinking what I'm thinking?"

"If you're thinking we should see if they're having an interest meeting soon, hell yea! There's something different about them than the other organizations, and I like being

different."

"I'm with you! Let's go see what they

say."

My brother and I walked over and introduced

ourselves to a brother by the name of Bro.

DipStick greeted us and told us if we were

interested in learning more about the fraternity

to give him our contact information and two

hours before the informational, we'd receive a

text message with where to be. We thought it

was a bit odd but since they piqued our interest,

we went along with it.

Three days later, just as I was leaving my

photography class, I get a text message with an

address and a message that read 'meet us at the address within the next hour and a half, turn your location on so we'll know when you have arrived.

"An hour and a half gives me enough time to shower, get dressed and get there," I said to myself.

Just as I was getting back to my apartment, my brother came right behind me.

"Did you get the text message too?" JayVon asked me.

"Yea, we need to shower, get dressed and be on our way, no time to bullshit."

"I already know what I'm wearing, and according to the GPS, it's twenty minutes from here and you know Atlanta traffic is like New York, so we gotta move it so we won't be late."

"Say less."

Jay and I pulled up with ten minutes to spare, one thing about us, we hated arriving somewhere right on time, which is something we got from our mother. When we got there, there were three other guys waiting to be let in.

"What's good fellas? I'm Justice, this is my twin brother JayVon."

"Peace king, I'm Daron," replied the one who was tall as hell.

"What's good Bruh, I'm André," replied another.

"What up y'all, I'm Levi, nice to meet y'all."

# The Freak in Me

JayVon replied, nice to meet y'all. I thought for sure there'd be more people here."

"So did we, Levi replied.

Just as Brotha DipStick was opening the door, another brotha was running up.

"My bad on my tardiness, he said to Brotha DipStick, "I'm Xavier", he said to the rest of us.

We each dapped him up and followed Brotha DipStick into a room where there were about five or six other guys from Beta Delta Mu.

# Saige the Gemini

## Refreshing Your Memory
## My Man My Abuser

### Qortni

I used to give a fuck, then I stopped; you see the life of a pastor's child is not all it's cracked up to be. I'm not perfect, shit far from it to be real.

My name is Qortni Monroe; I'm nineteen years old from New Haven, one of the meanest cities in Connecticut, I recently dropped out of college 'cause I couldn't keep my scholarship money and change my major so I decided to just quit. I didn't just quit and do nothing with my life; I enrolled into a writing program that was strictly for writing and breaking into print.

# The Freak in Me

In 2004, a year after graduating from high school I met this guy by the name of Qamar Daniels and we began chatting through BlackPlanet, then Yahoo Messenger, then finally meeting in person.

On October 19, 2004, Qamar and I made it official, we officially became a couple. I officially was in a relationship with Satan himself and I wasn't even aware of what I was getting myself into. It still amazes me how someone can make himself or herself appear to be the best thing since sliced bread, but in all actuality they're the worst things since women getting their period once a month.

# Saige the Gemini

In the beginning everything between Qamar and I was real cool, conversations were always on point, we'd fall asleep on the phone with one another, 'cause neither one of us wanted to be the first to hang up; yeah, I used to do corny shit like that. Anyhow, his friends seemed to like me, as I think back on it now, maybe they liked me a little too much back then; they had a very unique way of getting to know me, a way that I didn't think too much of, and didn't think anything was wrong with how we began getting to know one another.

"So, Qortni, what's your sign?" Asked Qamar's cousin Nathan,

"I'm a sexy Gemini."

# The Freak in Me

"Cool, what's your favorite position?"

"Doggy style, all day every day."

"Damn, how come I couldn't have met you first? I don't think Qamar will know what to do with you or how to handle you, real talk," chimed in Nature.

Just as Nature was about to ask me a question, Qamar called for me.

"Qortni, let me holla at you for a minute," he said with a hint of aggravation in his voice.

"Excuse me guys, I'll be right back."

I left Nature and Nathan sitting on Qamar's sun porch and made my way into Qamar's mother's house.

# Saige the Gemini

"What's up bae? How come you sound irritated and mad?"

"Why the fuck are you out there telling these guys your favorite positions like it's all good?"

"They asked and I answered."

"You don't see anything wrong with you telling that type of shit to my cousin and peoples?"

"What the fuck is the big problem? You're acting like I'm outside fucking them; they're asking me questions, and I'm answering. What? You want me to not answer the questions when they ask me?" I asked with my hands on my hips and my neck rolling.

# The Freak in Me

"Don't you ever again in your life disrespect me like that again, do you understand me? If they ask you questions like that, you better tell them that you are not at liberty to divulge that type of information, do we understand each other?"

I began laughing, was he serious? "Last time I checked, I was a grown ass woman, I don't have a ring on my left ring finger, so if anyone wanted to ask me what ever questions they feel as they want an answer to, I will answer."

"You must think I'm joking," he said getting into my face and stepping into my personal space.

# Saige the Gemini

"I never said you were joking, but I want you to realize that as long as I'm not sucking their dicks or fucking them, I'm not being disrespectful. I'm merely having an adult conversation with them; now chill the fuck out," I told him before walking back out to the sun porch.

Nathan and Nature must've heard the conversation Qamar and I were having and thought it would be best if they left because they were nowhere in sight when I got back to the porch.

Being that they left, I decided to get my bag and bounce as well. Qamar really had some shit with him, so instead of staying over any longer I just thought it best to give him his time to cool off. I stepped into his mother's kitchen and as soon as I turned the corner into the kitchen, I was knocked on my ass, courtesy of Qamar and his left fist,

"What the fuck is your problem? Why in the hell did you punch me? Are you out of your mind?" I asked with the most perplexed look on my face.

"Oh, you must have thought you were goin' to have the last word and just go on about your business?"

"Do you realize you just put your fucking hands on me? Do you realize that by doing that you just signed your own death certificate? You

Saige the Gemini

spoke your piece, I spoke mine, and I waked

away, end of story."

"Nah shorty, it's not the end of the story

'til I say so," he told me, having the audacity to

try and help me up.

I pushed his hand away, getting up off the

floor by myself; I went to his mother's

bathroom and noticed my left eye was

beginning to swell. I retrieved my bag from the

kitchen and started to walk to the front door,

but noticed Qamar sitting on his mother's couch

with tears flowing freely from his eyes. I didn't

want to stop and ask what his problem was, but

seeing him cry, the little angel on my shoulder

told me not to be cold and ask him if he was all

right.

"What's the matter Q?"

# Tony

## *Back in New Jersey*

I knew I couldn't hide my marriage from Qortni forever but I didn't want her to find out like this. I felt like shit because I know the feelings Qortni possessed for me and I know how I feel about her. Never in a million years did I think I would end up married, but here I am.

My wife and I have known each other for just a short time but when you know it's right you make your move then. It was so hard and it hurt so much knowing that I couldn't tell Qortni the real reason I couldn't make it to the baby shower or to the hospital when she was in labor, my wife kept getting suspicious when I kept leaving to go out of town when I was going to visit Qortni and have my one on one time with Arisa when Qort was still pregnant with her, I had to cut my visits to CT down because my wife was starting to ask questions and believe it or not I didn't want to keep lying to her.

I know I won't be able to keep Arisa from my wife forever I just have to find the right time to tell her.

"Baby, you look like you have something on your mind, is everything all right?" my wife Talia asked me.

"There's something I need to tell you but I'm not too sure how you're going to take it."

"What do you need to tell me Tony?"
"Come sit down."

She sat across from me, "I'm sitting now, what's the matter?

"Remember how before we got married I would make frequent trips to Connecticut late at night? I wasn't going to see my brother, I was actually going to see my youngest child's mother, I would sit in the car with her and rub her belly and talk to our daughter."

"Your daughter? I thought you only had two children?"

"I had a baby girl two day before we got married, which is why I had to go to Connecticut the day before our wedding so my baby mother wouldn't trip, she had already cussed me out for missing the birth of our daughter. I knew if I went to Connecticut and stayed for a few days you would start to get suspicious."

"Why didn't you tell me about her sooner?"

"I didn't want to tell you before because I was afraid of losing you, I didn't know how you would react to it."

"So why did you decide to tell me now?"

"Because it's been eating me up inside knowing that I've been keeping this away from you, I knew I wasn't going to be able to keep it from you forever, I'm sorry."

"So, who's her mother?"

"Her name is Qortni, we used to date but there were some issues that kept us from continuing our relationship."

"Okay, this is a lot to process but I'm glad you told me and didn't continue to keep it from me."

"I'm hoping Qort and I can come to some type of agreement to get Arisa here for the weekends so she can interact with us, I want to form a bond with her, she's my baby girl."

"The next holiday is Thanksgiving and we'll be in New Haven so how about seeing if she'll be willing to allow the baby to come spend the evening with us, it's worth a try."

"That's why I love you, you always got my back and never judge me."

## Saige the Gemini

"We have to have each other's back baby; marriage is about compromise."

I didn't honestly think Talia would be as understanding as she was, I began to wonder if she was being too understanding, I don't know of any female who would be fine with knowing that her new husband had a brand new baby that was born just two days before they got married; I guess that's what makes Talia one of a kind.

I already knew Qortni wasn't going to agree with Arisa staying with me and my family for Thanksgiving, especially with my wife being there, I was going to have to try to work something out with her.

# The Freak in Me

## Qortni

Tony was married, he had a real ring on his finger, he had a wife, he was off the market. He hurt me, he betrayed my trust, and to say I was crushed by the news would be a total understatement. As much as I tried to convince myself that I wasn't still in love with Tony, I knew I was lying to myself.

Now all of his "something came up" moments finally made sense to me, he was preparing for his wedding that whole time. My heart felt like it was ripped right out of my body, I should have been numb to all of the hurt and pain I had endured over the past few years from Qamar and Tony, but hearing Tony admit that he was married was a totally different type of hurt and pain.

I started to wonder what his wife had that I didn't that made him choose her over me to be his bride. He knew damn well how I felt about him and it felt as if he just said, "fuck Qortni's feelings," and went about his business. I can tell you one thing though, I'll be damned if he thinks my daughter will be anywhere near his wife, I want to meet her before my daughter is ever in her presence; I'll be damned if that bitch tries to inflict any harm on my daughter because she's feeling some type of way about Tony having a baby who is two days older than their marriage.

## Qortni

## August 2009

Tony and I haven't been on the best of terms lately, he hasn't been around to see Arisa, he hasn't been helping out financially, he's been doing absolutely nothing and it's starting to really piss me off, he just doesn't care. The last time I talked to him was a few weeks ago, I needed him to come with me to the Department of Social Services so we could fill out the papers for child support. After almost a month of procrastinating on taking his portion of the paternity test, he finally did, so now we had to do the paperwork.

On my one day off from work I was spending it on Bassett Street at the Social Services building, not something I was looking forward to. Being that it was crowded in the building I decided to bring Arisa outside to get some fresh air since Tony hadn't even showed up yet. As I was playing with Arisa outside this guy that went to high school with my older brother happened to be walking up Bassett towards me, I think we noticed one another at the same time.

"Qort, long time no see, how have you been?"

"I've been good Markus, how have you been? How long have you been in town?"

# Saige the Gemini

"I just got in town night before last, you know I only stay for a short time, nothing but trouble here for me. Is this your little mama?"

"Yes, this is my baby girl Arisa," I told him while turning Arisa around so he could see her face.

"She's beautiful Qort, just like her mother," Markus told me with a wink.

Back in the day I had a major crush on Markus, he played basketball with my oldest brother when they were in high school, it was something about him that stood out to me more than the other guys.

"Thank you sweetie, well, her dad just pulled up, we gotta go in here and handle some stuff for your
Little lady."

"No doubt, get lil mama right. Give me your number so we can stay in contact, I can't

The Freak in Me

believe you're all grown up now with a baby of your own."

"Yeah I ain't little no more," I told him laughing. We exchanged numbers and he went on his merry way.

"Who the fuck was that Qort? All in your face and in my daughter's face, what the hell is up with that?"

"None of your damn business as to who that was, your business should be your wife, you remember her right? The chick you married two days after my daughter was born, now can we go handle our business please?"

"Why must she be so damn difficult? Aren't you glad I never acted like that towards you?" Tony's baby mother Camdyn asked him. I guess she thought I didn't hear her but I did, loud and clear.

"Listen bitch, what Tony and I discuss is between him and I, what the fuck are you doing here anyway? Last time I checked Tony didn't need a chaperone here with him to sign paperwork.

"I got your bitch, you young, insecure piece of shit."

Tony interjected, "Can we not do this today please? Like seriously, all of this isn't even necessary, y'all are acting real fucking childish and it's uncalled for."

I told him, "Tell that thirsty, dusty baby mama of yours to learn how to mind her business."

"Bitch you 'bout to make me run you a fair one, keep coming out of your mouth sideways towards me."

"Name the time and place shorty, you ain't saying nothing but a fuckin' word."

Tony shook his head and said, "Camdyn, you can leave now, I just needed a ride here and I specifically asked you not to start with Qortni today and you just couldn't keep your damn comments to yourself. You always trying to start some shit and it's not necessary."

"Fine Tony, have it your way, don't bother coming back over to the house after you finish with her," Camdyn replied as she rolled her eyes and walked off.

"Why would you even bring that bird with you?"

"Qort, please don't start. I asked her for a ride down here, that's all, I didn't even want her to get out of the car but she insisted, she said she wanted to see the baby."

"Whatever Tony, can we go in so we can get this stuff done today so I can go about my business, please?"

"Have it your way Qortni. You know, I was thinking, you know my birthday is coming up, how about you, me and Arisa go out to eat or something? I haven't really spent too much time with her."

"You just realized you haven't spent enough time with your daughter? I don't mind doing lunch afterward, you're paying though."

"How you gonna make me pay for my birthday lunch? And to answer your question, no, I didn't just realize I haven't been spending enough time with her, I've been realized it, I just don't want to be bothered with your smart-ass mouth every time I come to town to see her. We're going to have to come to some type of common ground when it comes to me spending time with my daughter. You know your family doesn't like me, so coming to your house to see her is out of the question."

"If you really wanted to see her, despite how my family feels about you, you would make an honest effort to see her, liker seriously, enough with the excuses, I'm tired of hearing them."

"We'll work something out and soon." We handled our business with Social Services and went out to lunch. I can't even front on y'all, it felt damn good being in Tony's presence again, regardless of how much we argue, disagree or stop talking to one another for any length of time, we always come back a little stronger. Being out to eat with him and our daughter soothed my heart, even if it was temporary; I knew sooner rather than later he would return to Jersey to be with his wife.

"So, have you told your wife about Arisa yet or is it still the elephant in the room at your house?"

"I told her, she wants me to see if it's possible for you to let Arisa come with me and my family to Thanksgiving Dinner this year, we'll be in Connecticut at my sister's house, my sister you met on my dad's side."

"Tony, you know that's not going to happen unless I meet your wife first, in person, one on one."

"Why do you need to meet her in person first, do you not trust her?"

"Honestly? I don't trust either one of you, and I don't trust your family and you know I don't like half of them anyway."

"It's not fair to keep my child away from her family on my side, she needs to get to know my side of the family Qort."

"It's not fair how they outcast her before she was even born, now either I meet your wife prior to Thanksgiving or my child spending the holidays with you is a no go, simple and plain."

"I'm telling you now, you're not going to meet Talia, that's never going to happen so get that out of your head now. You do know I can take you to court to get partial custody of Arisa right?"

"You know that in the state of Connecticut you are considered a deadbeat dad because you left me during the pregnancy right? So your chances of getting any type of custody of my child is nil to none, but please, by all means, try and go for it, I have all of your messages saved and ready to print out when you were cussing me out, telling me my child isn't yours and all of the derogatory things you said to me while I was pregnant with Arisa."

"Have it your way Qortni, I just want to be in my daughter's life, that's all, I don't want to keep arguing with you, I don't want to go weeks or months without seeing her, I just want to get to know her and have her get to know her father, am I asking for too much?"

"No, you're not asking too much but you have to realize something Tony, you haven't been the easiest person to get along with during my pregnancy, I don't fully trust you anymore, and you're going to have to prove to me why I should trust you again. You have hurt me time and time again and I haven't fully gotten over it. You think you can just walk out of my life and back in whenever you feel like it, it doesn't work like that; it's not fair to me or my child."

"I hear you Qort and for all the times I've hurt you, I do apologize, I just want to do right by Arisa, be there for you and her, that's all I want."

"Actions speak louder than words."

We ate our lunch and I rode around just so Tony could spend more time with Arisa. At times I felt as if I was too hard on Tony but then I would think about all of the broken promises he made me and made our daughter. When I was pregnant with Arisa, Tony would drive down at night to have his daddy/daughter time with her,

# The Freak in Me

he would talk to her, rub my belly and even bring me food at times; I wished those times would last forever.

There's no doubt that I love Tony, mainly because he gave me my first child but I'm still in love with him as well, you can't help who your heart falls in love with...

www.ingramcontent.com/pod-product-compliance
Lightning Source LLC
Chambersburg PA
CBHW060350030726
47497CB00003B/667